Praise for Miracle Girl

A poignant coming-of-age story, *Miracle Girl* takes readers on a journey through doubt, grief, and love, ending ultimately with faith and hope. Another thoroughly enjoyable read by Jennifer DiGiovanni. ~ Patricia B. Tighe, author of *Life in the No-Dating Zone*

An inspirational story of faith, first love, and refusing to allow others to define you, with captivating characters and a swoon worthy love interest, *Miracle Girl* delivers it all. ~ T.H. Hernandez, author of The Union Series

Other Titles by Jennifer DiGiovanni

Prom-Wrecked (with T.H. Hernandez)

Truth in Lies

Fire in Ice

My Senior Year of Awesome

My Junior Year of Loathing

My Sophomore Year of Rules

My Clueless Broken Heart

My Freshman Year of Fabulous

MIRACLE GIRL

JENNIFER DIGIOVANNI

Vinspire Publishing, LLC
www.VinspirePublishing.com

Book Design by Woven Red Author Services, www.WovenRed.ca

First Edition

ISBN: 978-1-7327112-9-7

Published by Vinspire Publishing, LLC

Library of Congress Cataloging-in-Publication Data
DiGiovanni, Jennifer, author
Miracle Girl
Ladson, South Carolina: Vinspire Publishing [2019]
Library of Congress Control Number:2019946344
BISAC: YOUNG ADULT FICTION/RELIGIOUS/CHRISTIAN/RELATIONSHIPS

To my parents
—for teaching me about faith

Chapter 1

When the clock strikes ten on the eve of June eighth, the floodlights surrounding my house switch on, throwing a glare in my room. And so the annual ritual begins. Somewhere close by, Dad's phone rings and he barks out a rushed hello.

Night air pushes through the screen in my window, moving the curtains and giving me a glimpse of the truck beeping as it backs into the driveway. The rear door clanks open and a ramp falls out. Two men unload wire fencing and painted signs, calling to each other as they assemble a barricade to hold back the incoming crowds, threatening to trample our lawn. I turn on my white noise machine and select the ocean setting, drowning out the distraction with a calming sound. A semester's worth of history notes sit in front of me, but the words seem to blur together and lose their meaning.

Dad's voice rises above the commotion; there's an edge of exhaustion cutting through his carefully composed tone. He's spent most of the day declining media requests and dealing with angry neighbors. The residents of Chestnut Street despise the complications of June eighth. Reaching over my desk, I yank the shade down, but the taunting floodlights still creep through the one inch gap.

"Leanne?" Mom taps on my bedroom door before pushing it open. "Is Callie picking you up in the morning?"

"With the traffic detours, she won't have time." Leaning back in my chair, I twist my hair into a knot on the top of my head. Then I poke my pencil through the heavy coil—my favorite at-home hairstyle. "I'll set my alarm early and walk through the woods." *Or run.* "Sister Bernadette said I could wait in the library until class starts."

Mom steps closer, glancing at the notes spread over my desk. "Are you ready for this to be over?"

I'm not sure if she means exams, the school year...or just the next twenty-four hours. My anxiety has been growing for weeks and I'm about ready to capsize under the stress of June eighth.

Squeezing my shoulder, she breathes a quiet sigh. "Maybe this year will be better for you."

"Yeah. Maybe." I pick up a yellow highlighter, hoping to regain my focus for one last hour of studying. "It's not that I don't appreciate everything—"

"I'm not saying that. I know this is hard for you." Mom glances toward the window. "The attention. News cameras. All of it."

We rehash this same awkward conversation every June eighth eve. It's a Strong family tradition, like decorating the Christmas tree.

When I dare a glance at my mother, I notice the redness in her eyes. My fingers tighten around the highlighter until my knuckles turn white. I hate when she cries. She remembers a time when I was not the person I am today and I hate that too.

"You're truly a miracle, Leanne," she whispers.

Miracle. The word makes me cringe, even though the label is somewhat accurate. I'm Leanne Strong, the girl who was born with a debilitating spinal defect which doctors predicted would cause constant pain and make walking difficult. Not exactly the life my parents envisioned for their only child, born after years of infertility.

Mom moves to the bed and fluffs a pillow, trying to act as if she's not hovering. "Go right to school in the morning. Ask Callie for a ride home."

I'm only half-listening as my eyes zip down a list of World War II battles. "Okay."

"Keep your phone with you. I downloaded that new location app. If you run into trouble, text me and I'll find you."

"Stop worrying, Mom." I heave an exasperated breath. "Who'd hurt me on June eighth?"

She turns down my blankets, her mouth pressed into a thin line. "No one would purposely hurt you. But with all the excitement...I worry. It's what moms do."

In fact, my mother's abundance of concern is the reason June eighth is such an event in the town of Spring River. Fifteen June eighth eves ago, she kissed me goodnight, placed me in my crib, and said a quick prayer while holding a relic she'd received as a gift from a visiting priest. The relic was made of fabric taken from the robe of Saint Piera, back when she was designated as "blessed," meaning she'd been credited with one miracle by the Catholic Church. Mom left the piece of cloth on a table in my room and snapped off the light.

The next morning I woke with a loud cry. Actually, scream might be a better description. Mom rushed in to pick me up, convinced I was suffering from excruciating pain. Instead, she found me standing in my crib, the first time I'd ever put weight on my legs.

It was a big deal.

The Vatican investigated and validated my medical miracle. Three years later, the Pope elevated Mother Piera to sainthood and invited my parents to fly with me to Rome to attend the ceremony, known as a canonization. I have only a blurry memory of these events, including a noisy Saint Peter's Square packed with people and my father lifting me up on his shoulders as everyone recited prayers under a bright blue sky.

Fifteen years later, it's still a big deal. Mom and Dad do their best to shield me from worldwide attention for three hundred and sixty-four days out of the year. Most of the time, my one claim to fame is forgotten, except for the framed magazine cover hanging in our living room. But on June eighth, everything wondrous and awe-inspiring about my miracle cure rushes back into our lives.

Since that long ago night, my life has been tied to a woman I never met, who lived half a world away and died fifty years before I was born. But now...we're forever linked by something that may have simply been the most epic of all coincidences.

Rarely do I get through an entire day without asking myself why this happened. If you passed me on the street, you'd say I'm nothing special. Miraculous healing aside, I'm completely unexceptional. I've been told my hazel eyes and long brown hair are a pretty combination, but my best friend Callie gets way more attention from boys. To be honest, I'm not a super brainiac or an athlete. Breaking a ten-minute mile in gym class was the highlight of my running life.

So how did I capture a famous saint's attention?

I wish I knew.

Because in the last fifteen years, I've learned just how lucky I am. Billions of people walk this Earth every day, waiting for some kind of miracle. Most of the time, it never comes.

~

Bang! *Pray for us, Leanne!*

Like magic, the June eighth choir appears, springing to life with an early-morning cymbal crash. I'm awake at 5:30 am, a time I wasn't sure existed outside of news reports and fairy tales.

Bang! My bed shakes. They brought a drum. Tambourines. Did someone roll an organ into my front yard?

As more voices join in the song, I scramble out of bed, intent on finding a way to escape before all my exit strategies disappear. Today's not a good day to take a long, hot shower, so I scrub soap on my face and throw my hair in a ponytail as I wish for an early tropical storm. Hailstones. A tornado warning. Any huge weather event will suffice. Something to keep the multitudes away.

"*Pray for me, Leanne Strong*!"

Our front door creaks open.

"Welcome, everyone," my father says in a somber voice. "Thank you for celebrating with us today. My daughter Leanne appreciates your prayers and well wishes." As Dad continues his carefully prepared speech, my pulse begins to pound. I grab my summer uniform from the closet: a pleated gray skirt, a white polo shirt and white knee socks which I tug as high as they'll go. The drumbeat kicks up again, followed by the wah-wah-wah of an electric guitar. Laughter bubbles in my chest, rising through my panic. The neighbors must be loving this early-morning Christian rock concert.

Mom pokes her head in my room. "Leanne, you should wait this out. The crowd's bigger than last year."

I shove my feet into a pair of loafers, my school shoes.

"Just...distract them. I can't miss my history final."

Our house phone rings and Mom hurries to answer. While she's occupied, I race down the stairs, toward the back door. I shoulder my backpack and pry the door open with my fingers. So far, the visitors have stayed in the front of my house, held back by the temporary fence. The back yard is still empty and a line of pine trees shields me from the view of the crowd.

The blare of a siren approaches, signaling the arrival of someone important. Hopefully someone who's willing to talk to the reporters congregating on the lawn.

I fill my lungs with a deep breath, then take off, sprinting through our neighbors' backyards.

The warmth of a late spring breeze sticks to my skin, weighing me down. At the end of the block, I dart around Mrs. Catterwaller's garage just as a white news van screeches through the crosswalk and brakes into a whiplash-inducing stop. A tall, thin lady wearing clicky heels jumps out. How did she see me? She can't possibly recognize—

"Leanne Strong!"

I duck behind Mrs. C.'s white Cadillac, my pulse pounding.

"She's here! Roll film."

Like a lion circling its prey, the reporter stalks closer, holding the mic out in front of her. Trapped between the Cadillac and Mrs. Catterwaller's garage door, my hands start to shake. The reporter waves her mic in front of my face. "Can you give us a few words, Leanne?"

Pieces of wind-blown hair whip out of my ponytail, falling over my face, though the reporter's blond blow-out looks fossilized. She's older than my mom, but with fewer wrinkles and a heck of a lot more makeup.

I sling my backpack around and hold it in front of my face.

"No comment."

Before she presses for an answer, I lunge past her, into the street, running in front of the news van and squeezing between two houses.

"Come back, Leanne! You've inspired so many! We want you to tell the story in your own words."

"Please leave me alone. I was a baby," I call over my shoulder. "I don't remember anything." Desperation kicks in, propelling me up and over the Murrays' split rail fence.

Overhead, the blades of a helicopter gnaw at the blue sky. Breathing heavily, I veer around the back of the Murrays' house, my heavy shoes clomping over the grass, heading for the safety of the woods. Helicopters can't fly through trees. Reporters won't find me in the twisted maze of dirt trails.

The familiar sign for the Spring River Nature Park appears, a welcome sight to anyone seeking refuge from the multitudes on Chestnut Street. In the distance, a voice speaks my name, amplified by a megaphone. I glance back and stumble, catching my foot on an exposed root. My ankle twists and I throw my hands out to break my fall. The sharp edge of a stone cuts my palm and a fallen branch scrapes my knee. I end up flat on the grass, whimpering.

I would've been home free if Mr. and Mrs. Murray bothered to take care of their yard.

Thwack.

Fear strikes me like an arrow piercing dead center through my heart. I push up from the ground and brush a leaf off my grass-stained uniform shirt.

Thwack.

Slowly, I turn, holding my backpack like a shield, and find an unfamiliar boy watching me, his brown eyes blazing under lowered brows. The breeze ruffles his hair, messing up what's already a haphazard style, at best. He's taller than me, with broad shoulders that look slightly misplaced on his thin frame.

Also: he's not a Murray.

Head tilted, he squints in the bright morning sun.

I raise one finger to hold him until I catch my breath. "You never saw me," I gasp.

He flips a baseball into the glove on his right hand. I flinch at the loud thwack.

"Are you the reason for the helicopter search?" He flips the ball again. *Thwack.*

Letting my backpack drop to the ground, I bend forward and place my hands on my knees, still heaving from a combination of overexertion and anxiety. "Possibly," I manage to say.

"Cool. What'd you do? Rob a bank?" *Thwack.*

He doesn't know who I am. Finally, something works in my favor.

Lifting a shoulder, I assume a look of innocence. "Don't worry about it. I mean, I'm not a criminal."

Another glance my way, followed by a scowl. "Sure you're not." *Thwack.*

Out on the street, blue and red lights flash as the sheriff's car zooms by. A trumpet blasts in the distance and a loud chorus of amens rises like a plume of smoke above the treetops. Sweat rolls from the nape of my neck, down my spine.

Keeping my eyes on the scowling boy, I tighten the strap on my backpack and turn back toward the woods. "I'd explain everything, but I really need to go. If Sheriff Wilson asks about me, you can tell him I left for school."

With a quick wave, I dart into the forest.

Chapter 2

Sister Bernadette and I have an unspoken arrangement. Whenever I need a break from reality, she lets me escape inside her books. In return, I help out around the library before and after school.

Last June eighth, my first year at Holy Family High, Sister found me cowering in the reference section, reapplying lip gloss after cutting through the nature trail on my way to school. Rather than asking why I wasn't reveling in my miraculousness, Sister raised an eyebrow and directed me into her office, which smells like stale coffee, dry ink, and dusty book jackets. She plunked her super-sized mug on the desk, opened a drawer and pulled out her secret stash of powdered donuts. Breaking open the box, she admitted she sometimes wears white blouses to hide the evidence of her favorite before-school snack. I wasn't sure if I was supposed to laugh at that, but I did.

"Isn't this an important day for you?" she asked while the sugar molecules danced in the air around us.

I extracted a tissue from the box in front of me and wiped

my lips. "It's the anniversary of my..." I couldn't bring myself to say the word, though it was obvious Sister knew what I was talking about.

"And you're hiding in the library?" Her blue eyes, the color of faded denim, swept from my head to my toes.

My chin lowered. "It's a lot of attention."

"Yes, I suppose it is." One side of her mouth moved up and down as she chewed. "Miss Strong, I shall pray for you."

Her remark put an immediate halt to my donut scarf-down. Most people, especially those of a religious nature, believe I've received my fair share of prayer fulfillment and then some. When Sister offered this new appeal to God, I felt...unworthy.

But I wasn't about to argue her point and risk losing my chance at nabbing future donuts. So I bowed my head and said, "Thank you, Sister."

"Anytime, Miss Strong. My prayers are free of charge." Pinching her lips together, she studied me for a long minute. A lock of silver-blond hair slid across her forehead and she pushed it back with a deliberate movement. "Though if you'd like to properly demonstrate your gratitude, I have a cart filled with returns waiting to be shelved."

Thus began our mutually beneficial librarian/student assistant relationship. Sister Bernadette is the only Catholic school teacher I've met who has never, not one time, offered me up as an example of the power of God. She rarely makes reference to my exceptionality. Instead, she prefers to discuss her latest book shipment.

So exactly one year later, when I saunter into the library at 6:23 a.m., Sister is waiting for me. She hoists her mug of hazelnut-flavored coffee in the air. Someone donated an outdated Keurig to the school last year and believe me, the library gang loves their K-cups.

I jam a hot chocolate pod into the machine and slide a paper cup under the dispenser. "Good morning, Sister. May I hang out in here?"

She nods and gives me the once-over, taking special note of my wrinkled, stained shirt. "Did you run into trouble this morning?"

The Keurig spits out my drink and I settle carefully into a bean bag chair, warm cup in hand, inhaling the decadence of powdered chocolate. "Nothing more than my typical June eighth travels." I pull out my phone and text Mom, letting her know I made it to school without any major incidents.

Sister leans in, nostrils flaring. In addition to dirt smudges and grass stains, my uniform contains more than a trace of sweat, irritating her highly sensitive olfactory system. She sighs and reaches for her remote. "Might as well watch the festivities until class starts."

The TV mounted on the wall flickers to life. An image of my now densely populated front yard appears.

"Your mother's rhododendrons are gorgeous," Sister Bernadette says, admiring the purple blooms popping up behind the yellow police tape.

"She won't trim them until after today. No sense working on plants when someone might crush them trying to get close to the house."

Monsignor Mainworthy, pastor of Saint Genevieve Parish, stands next to a younger priest I've never seen before today. The television reporter who'd chased me down an hour ago holds her microphone in front of their faces.

"This year, in honor of the 15th anniversary of the Leanne Strong miracle, we are proud to announce the opening of a holy shrine in Spring River," says the younger priest, whose glasses are fogged over from the humidity. "Construction will be completed by the end of the summer and at that time, the Archbishop plans to attend our most sacred dedication."

"Will Miss Strong attend the opening ceremony?" the reporter asks.

Beside me, Sister Bernadette snickers. "Opening ceremony. This is the Catholic Church, not the Olympics."

Monsignor leans past the younger priest, reaching for the microphone. "Absolutely. Miss Strong will be present to pay homage to the most holy saint who performed such a wondrous miracle."

A murmur rolls through the crowd.

I bobble my drink, nearly spilling hot chocolate in my lap. What's he talking about? Apparently, I make appearances now. Glaring at the TV, I say, "No one bothered to ask me about this."

Sister eyes me as she carefully peels an orange. "Given that the shrine will be located less than five miles from your house, I think it's safe to assume you'll be in attendance. You don't want to make a liar out of Monsignor, do you?"

"No, of course not." I dig my fingernails into the bean bag's vinyl fabric. "Do I even have a choice?"

After tossing a piece of orange rind in the small garbage can under her desk, Sister says, "Yes, Leanne. You have a choice. Faith is a choice."

I swallow hard and drop my voice to a whisper. "What happened to me didn't have anything to do with my personal faith. My mother believed. Not me."

"Then choose to make an appearance because you believe in your mother. You're a living, breathing sign of her faith." Sister clicks the remote, cutting off Monsignor's rather long-running oration. "I keep an extra uniform shirt in my coat closet. You'll need to change before Principal Daniels sees you. And there's a cart of books ready to shelve outside my office. It should keep you busy until homeroom."

~

"Sheesh, it's a jungle out there. The cops asked for my student ID before they let me pull into the parking lot." Callie rushes into homeroom at the last minute and slaps her backpack on the desk. "Happy Miracle Day!" She swivels her neck and her blond curls flow like moveable artwork. "Oops. Sorry, I forgot how much you hate the m-word."

Keeping my head down, I open my notebook and doodle a bunch of circles. "I don't hate the word. I just don't understand why today has become a worldwide celebration, as such."

"I wouldn't define it as a worldwide celebration. More like a highly localized carnival. There's at least four news trucks in the parking lot. One of them has a giant pole to send pictures to satellites."

"Who nabbed the TV interview this year?" Usually one of my distant acquaintances manages to convince the paparazzi that we're best friends and reveals some unfounded truth about me. Something ridiculous like my ability to levitate over cafeteria tables for fun.

"Mandy Stewert. Apparently, she had a cold last month and when you touched her it went away."

"Is that why she sat at our lunch table for three days straight?" Anger spikes in my chest. Mandy and I played soccer together for six years before she decided to focus on dance and I stepped away from team sports. We did the playdate thing all through elementary school. She knows me well enough to understand how much I hate being called out for my supposed exceptionality. "If I could perform miracles, I wouldn't be sitting here, waiting to take my history final. I'd be flying over Spring River, on my way to the beach."

Callie rests her hand on my arm. A trail of red scratches stretches from her wrist to her elbow.

"What happened to you?"

"Oh, the cat got me again."

I press my fingers on the marks. "See? No miracle forthcoming."

"I guess a few scratches aren't worthy of divine intervention." She draws her hand away.

"Did you get a summer job yet?" I ask, desperate to change the subject.

"I'm working at the day camp, remember? They're still looking for another assistant counselor. Any interest?"

"I don't think so. I'm working for my dad again." Running a one-lawyer firm in a small town limits the number of full-time staff in Dad's budget. He saves mountains of legal documents for my annual eight-week organize-the-office binge. And being that Dad's not a technology buff by any stretch of the imagination, I've got some plans to modernize his filing system this year while I'm at it.

Callie presses the back of her hand to her forehead. "Another summer wasting away, standing in front of the copy machine? C'mon, you can do better than that, Leanne. We need to have fun."

"We'll have fun after work. We have our summer movie list, remember?"

"Sure, but I hoped this year we wouldn't be the only two people in the theater for the late night shows."

"It's a nice dream, but unlikely," I say, though I can't help wondering if watching a string of one-star films would be as much fun with anyone but Callie. "And your job isn't all flirting and fun, you know."

"Yeah, yeah, kids can be tough. Always trying to run away and stuff. That's why the counselors work in groups." Callie twists one of her long curls around her finger. "When the sun is shining and you're stuck in that stuffy office you know you'll be jealous."

I raise an eyebrow. "Jealous? Of you?"

"Darn right. I'll be getting tan and hanging out with cute guys. You'll be faxing and copying with your boring dad."

"Dad's not boring." But I hear the lack of conviction in my voice.

Callie rolls her eyes. "Puh-leaze. Every good dad is boring. It's part of the job description. When they try to be fun—that's when you know something's not right with the world."

I shut my notebook and stuff it into my backpack, anxious to move on as soon as the next bell rings. Six classes, lunch, and a study period bring me that much closer to June ninth.

"By the way, how's your dad? Still going through a midlife crisis?" I ask, using Callie's euphemistic term to describe her father's behavior. She rarely talks about her parents, but I know they've had some ups and downs after her dad recently lost his job.

Callie starts to answer, but before she can update me, Mrs. Boyle enters the room and laser beams a gaze my way. "Good morning, everyone." I bend forward and retie my shoelace in a triple knot. "Leanne, would you like to lead us in prayer on this special day?"

Cue the snide laughter from the boys in the back of the classroom. We've spent enough years in school together. By now, they know how my June eighth works.

I shuffle to the front of the room, keeping my eyes trained

on the floor. Mrs. Boyle beams as she hands me a laminated card and I recite a prayer to Saint Piera. After a half-hearted round of amens from the class, I return to my seat and flip through my history notes as the morning announcements play through the speakers.

The bell rings, and we move on to our first class. I manage to power through my history exam, but the effects of my early wake-up call quickly settle in. Callie hooks her arm through mine, forcing me to keep up as we move through the halls between classes. I yawn a hello to the Girlfriends, a clique of the more popular girls Callie and I are friendly with, although we tend to hang on the fringe of their social circle. They're not mean girls by any stretch of the imagination; it's more that we're interested in different things. They dance competitively, star in school shows, and run student council fundraisers. I read and work in the library. Callie plays field hockey and basketball.

In Honors Theology, Callie is waiting for me, ready to chat about her exam grades, which most teachers have already posted online, before we all mentally check out for the summer. For the rest of the day, we plan to flip through yearbooks, send texts from our phones concealed under the desks, and delete any incriminating information from our school laptops before we turn them in for the summer. For a while, I return to my normal high school bubble. But, eventually, the reminders about what's going on outside creep in.

"Miracle Girl's here," someone whispers when I pop in the bathroom to tighten the elastic band around my ponytail.

"Right over there." A junior points me out to a freshman when I stop by my locker for a forgotten text book.

"No halo today, Miss Strong?" Mr. Lee, the new math teacher, smiles when we pass each other in the hallway. This is our first June eighth together. I duck my head, feeling my cheeks grow warm. Is he seriously expecting a mystical event?

"So, think about the camp job," Callie says, as I try to ignore my growling stomach for one more class before lunch. I should've grabbed an extra donut from Sister Bernadette. "The guys probably won't know you're famous. At least, I promise not to tell them. You can be just Leanne for one summer."

We enter the science lab and take our seats. She turns to her lab partner, ready to discuss the final grade on their research project, and I realize I forgot to tell her the news about the shrine. No matter what Callie says, somehow I know this summer will be anything but normal.

Chapter 3

By the time I arrive in the cafeteria and buy my usual slice of pizza and carton of chocolate milk, everyone seems to have forgotten about June eighth. We have summer plans to discuss and end-of-the-year parties to organize.

But out on the blacktop, the line of cameras aimed at the school building is hard to ignore. Applause breaks out at a table in the corner when a brave freshman runs through the parking lot and photo bombs the live news update.

"Why are they still here?" With my chin propped in my hands, I watch reporters calling in updates, camera crews setting up their equipment, and assistants holding poles with microphones attached. "Don't they need my permission to take a picture?"

Callie dives into her cheese and tomato sandwich. "Maybe the reporters think you're something like...a public figure. Or a movie star—but only for one day a year."

After a school-wide prayer service gets me out of my last sophomore gym class, thanks to Saint Piera, Callie and I sit in the back of the classroom during our study period to work on an escape plan. She turned sixteen last December and already has her license, plus her dad gave her his old Jeep, saving me from another sprint through the woods.

When the final bell rings, Callie makes a break for the student lot. I stuff my hair under a baseball cap and hide between two dumpsters overflowing with the remains of four hundred student lunches. Luckily, a bus filled with missionary students pulls into the parking lot, blocking me from the cameras when they join the festivities. The doors swing open and kids pour out of the building, smiling and waving. Everyone wants to be on TV. I poke my head around the side of the dumpster and spy Callie's Jeep pulling into the traffic lane. When she closes in, I jump out from my hiding spot as Callie hits the breaks and the tires squeal to a stop.

Prying open the side door, I scoot inside. "Go for it!"

The Jeep shoots forward, catching up to the car in front of us before anyone notices her extra passenger.

"Should we say hi to your fan club?" She pokes her hand through the open roof and blasts the horn. Heads turn in our direction, but the reporters are held back by a wall of people waving to the cameras. Callie pumps up the radio volume to full blast and cackles like the Wicked Witch flying away on her broom. We veer out of the parking lot, with the reporters giving chase, calling my name.

At the end of the school zone, Callie presses the gas pedal. "If they only knew the real you. The girl who hid behind the bleachers to get out of playing volleyball in gym class."

I wince at the memory. "Who never finishes her math homework on time."

"The girl who falls asleep during first period on a regular basis, then denies it when questioned," Callie continues.

"The girl who'll never live up to the hype," I finish.

"Amen, sister. Your miracle hype is way overrated. Where do you want me to drop you off?"

"On Brighton Avenue. I'll hop a fence and run through the backyards."

She swerves the wheel, following my direction. "You'd rather cut through a bunch of strangers' yards than risk a run-in with a news camera?"

"If the strangers aren't trying to take my picture, then yes." I tug my baseball cap lower to shade my eyes. "Stop...right...now!"

Callie brakes and I roll out of the Jeep, swinging my backpack over my shoulder. "Thanks for the ride."

"Anytime, friend," she calls, already driving away.

Before anyone recognizes me, I vault over a fence, run between two swing sets and circumvent a trampoline. When I press open the back gate and enter my yard, only a single news van waits in front of my house. I hide behind Mom's potted tomato plants until the two men with cameras crane their necks to check a car zooming down Chestnut Street. Taking advantage of the split-second distraction, I dart through the back door.

"Mom!" I stomp into the mudroom and rip off my baseball hat, shoving it my backpack. "What the heck is going on? Who's building a shrine in Spring River? And who said I agreed to participate in the dedication? As if!"

"Hello, Leanne. Did you have a nice day at school?" Mom calls to me from the kitchen in her fake-cheery voice. Which means...she's not alone. I picture my rude remarks quoted on the front page of tomorrow's Spring River Times.

Skirting into the kitchen, I pause in the doorway, pushing up on my toes. Seated around the table, I spot another mom-like figure with blond hair and round glasses, slightly taller and heavier than my own parental model. Next to her sits a boy with dark brown hair, longer on top, deep brown eyes and a square jaw. Though their coloring is different, the two share a resemblance in the shape of their faces and their hesitant smiles. My eyes scroll over the boy's short-sleeved T-shirt, noting the extreme muscle definition in his arms. All three of them turn to me and I snap my eyes away from the boy, back to my mother. Mouth falling open, I start to ask a question, but stop. Am I in trouble? Why did Mom let someone cross the police line?

The silence lasts long enough that my toes start to numb. I drop my heels to the floor and catch the boy eyeing me with a curious stare. Instant recognition knocks at my brain. He's the baseball boy. The guy who caught me trespassing in the Murray's backyard this morning. Did he tell someone about my escape?

Air freezes in my chest. I wonder if the boy was an undercover spy. Maybe his mother is a reporter. Possibly a police investigator. Or, even worse, a representative from the Vatican.

"Leanne, this is Patti Dalisay and her son Braeden." Mom rises to her feet and speaks in a breezy voice. "They moved into the Murrays' house last week and couldn't help but notice the activity in the neighborhood this morning."

"We wanted to ask if we could do anything to help. All those people...it must be scary for you," Mrs. Dalisay adds.

"Oh, we're used to it by now." Mom's false laugh conveys her discomfort. "Actually, *we* should be knocking on your door to welcome you to the neighborhood. Right, Leanne?"

"Oh, right. Exactly. Um, hi?" I say, unsure why my words sound like a question. "I didn't know the Murrays' place was for sale."

"My husband works with their oldest son," Mrs. Dalisay explains. "We toured the house before they put it on the market and fell in love with Chestnut Street."

"The Murrays retired to Florida last month," Mom adds. "Didn't I tell you?"

I shrug. Mr. and Mrs. Murray were ancient and not the nice friendly old couple you'd imagine when you think of two silver-haired people married for fifty years. They kept to themselves unless a dog got loose on their property. Then it was World War III against the neighbors.

"So, this is Leanne." Mrs. Dalisay's bright green eyes travel from the top of my loose ponytail to my white knee socks. "I'm delighted to meet you." And honestly, with her super bright smile, Mrs. Dalisay does appear incredibly delighted. "The Murrays never mentioned anything about living so close to the site of the Spring River miracle."

Mom coughs out another jittery laugh. "We weren't very friendly with the Murrays. The crowds we see this time of year tend to cause a lot of commotion around here, so I can understand why they didn't tell you about us."

"If you ask me, miracles are worth celebrating, even if they cause a slight disruption. We loved all the excitement." Mrs. Dalisay turns to her son. "Right, Braeden?"

He who is named Braeden lifts a shoulder, setting off a rippling motion through his upper arm muscles. "It was cool until the helicopter pilot almost crashed into our roof when the wind picked up."

While Mrs. Dalisay does a double take, looking somewhat horrified by her son's answer, I widen my eyes and tilt my head, silently tossing him my eternal gratitude. He must have covered for me this morning, because I made it the rest of the way to school without interference.

Braeden responds by lowering his eyelids halfway, appearing bored by this whole situation.

"Do you have any other children, Patti?" asks Mom.

Mrs. Dalisay pauses for a beat. "My daughter Sami is helping my husband unpack. I didn't want to overwhelm you, so I just brought Braeden."

Mom steps closer to me and wraps her arm around my shoulders, nudging me toward our guests. "Leanne and I are so happy you stopped by, especially today. It's nice to have a little normalcy, especially after this morning. The crowd seems to grow every year."

"I'm sure this is a busy day for you. We should go." Mrs. Dalisay pushes back from the table and Braeden follows.

"Why don't you use the back door?" Mom lifts a bakery box off the counter. "I'll take these cupcakes to our visitors and talk to them while you sneak across the street." The moms share a smile and march away, chatting like long-lost friends.

"Thanks for helping me out today," I whisper to Braeden as he passes by.

"I didn't do anything," he whispers back to me.

"I know. That's why I said thanks. You could have talked to the reporter about me."

His brow creases. "Why would I do that?"

I lean back, resting my shoulder blades against the wall. "People like to be on TV. It makes them feel important, or famous, or—"

"Not me." He abruptly turns away, following his mother. "See you around, Leanne."

Compared to the kids in school falling over each other to nab interviews, Braeden's behavior seems odd. I thought everyone wanted to be famous. Except me.

The side door clicks shut and I breathe a sigh of relief. I'm pouring a glass of milk when Mom returns, brimming with excitement over our new neighbors.

I stow the milk carton in the refrigerator and tap the door closed. "Why did you sign me up for this shrine thing? You know I don't make public appearances."

She holds up her hand to halt my brewing tantrum. "I know how much you hate being a miracle poster child, but I think this time you really need to say yes. The shrine is a great honor for the town. Monsignor was practically doing a happy dance in our front yard."

"It's obviously a very big deal. The shrine coverage cut my usual June eighth camera time by at least thirty percent."

"Leanne, shush." Mom's eyes flick to the open window, like she fears someone might overhear my complaints. "Let's remember, it's not all about you. Yes, the shrine is being built in Spring River because this is where the miracle occurred. But Saint Piera has a large following in this area."

"Then let it be about her," I wail. "Not about me! Tell the church to build a shrine in Italy."

Mom opens the pantry and hands me a granola bar, most likely assuming my anger is exacerbated by low blood sugar. She's a certified nutritionist and everything comes back to food for her. "Actually, there is a shrine in Italy. The Church felt there should also be one in the United States."

"Who made that decision? I hardly think the Church cares that much about my miracle." Mom stays silent, knowing better than to argue. I toss the uneaten granola bar on the counter. "Did you tell whoever's building this shrine that I'm going to college in two years? Somewhere far away, where I'm not Leanne Strong, the girl who was miraculously cured. I want to be Leanne, the nice, normal girl who lives a nice, normal life. If I'm on TV during the dedication, it might make national news." I lower my voice and shoot Mom a pleading look. "The whole country will know what I look like. I'm the only person at school who's not on Snapchat or Instagram, because I'm trying to protect my identity, but now I'll never hide from this—this June eighth stuff."

Mom's eyes start to mist. "I know how much you hate the attention, Leanne. But, unfortunately, I don't think you'll ever be able to hide from it completely."

Okay, now I feel horrible. I hate, hate, hate when Mom cries. "Maybe not hide from it," I grumble. "But it can't be the only thing people know about me. When people only know me as a miracle child, they make false assumptions."

"Has someone spread a rumor about you? What did they say?"

I lift the cool glass of milk and press it to my forehead. My June eighth migraine has arrived. "They claim I walk on water. Cure the common cold. Turn water into wine. Stuff like that."

Mom laughs. "Walk on water, no. Six years of swimming lessons cost me a small fortune. And you'd better not be hiding any alcohol-related magic tricks from me."

A weak smile breaks out on my face. "Don't worry. I'd tell you about the wine thing."

She drops her eyes to the stack of June eighth newspapers sitting on the counter. She buys extra copies every year for her memory box. "Some people need to believe, Leanne. You bring them hope."

"They need to understand the truth, though. People show up at our house and assume I can fix their problems. Everyone's so grabby—like if they cut off a piece of me, they'll have part of my miracle."

"You can't pass faith like that. But your presence at the shrine might help people in ways you never imagined."

"How? I'm not the one who performs miracles."

"No, not yet," Mom agrees, to which I gag. "But you're Leanne. And I think there's something in you that you haven't discovered." She tucks a loose lock of my hair behind my ear. "Stop worrying about what everyone else in the world thinks, and concentrate on being yourself. No one is asking for more than that."

When I notice the tired lines around her eyes, I nod. "I'll try." I need to let this go. It's been a long day for both of us.

She picks up my glass and sets it in the sink. "So what did you think of our new neighbors?"

Braeden's face pops in my head and a weird sensation bubbles up from my stomach into my chest. "They seem okay." I won't tell my mother that my two main thoughts about Braeden Dalisay are one, that he's extremely attractive and two, very hard to figure out. In my mind, this is a scary combination.

Mom's eyebrows lift. "I thought they were nice. Maybe we should invite them over for dinner. After all, they did brave the June eighth hoopla to check on us."

"Okay, but I wouldn't rush into anything." My guess is a night with Braeden would be incredibly awkward and I'm not sure I'm willing to put myself through that, even though his mother appears sweet and nice.

But Mom smiles, undeterred. She needs a new friend and Patti Dalisay appears to be a prime candidate. "You're right. We'll give them a few days to settle in before I haul out my welcome wagon."

Chapter 4

Stories about the shrine fill the front page of the Spring River Times. Hotels will be built for the tourists. Restaurants and bars will be added along Main Street. Celebrities will visit, bringing more news cameras to our small town. The heaviness in my chest grows as I scan the articles.

"Breakfast, Leanne?" Mom slides a bowl of granola in front of me while I study a mock-up of the shrine and bell tower, designed to mimic a Mediterranean church with stone walls and a red-tiled roof.

"Did you see the statue?" Leaning over my shoulder, Mom points to the courtyard in front of the shrine, where twin fountains stand on either side of a statue of Saint Piera cradling a baby in her arms.

I hold the picture close and squint at the stone child's wispy locks of hair, shy smile, and heart-shaped face. "That's not me, is it?"

Mom shrugs, revealing nothing. "I might scan this page and add it to your website."

"I'd look into copyright issues first," I say, hoping to discourage her. My mother manages my internet page, but, really, any updates to leannestrong.com only appear by a twist of fate or if she repeatedly clicks the mouse until her laptop surrenders.

When I set the paper aside, Mom sets it on top of her junk mail pile at the end of the countertop. "I'll ask your father before I upload anything. Still, it's a beautiful building, isn't it?"

Picking up my spoon, I force down a mouthful of granola. "It's a pretty picture. But the shrine probably won't look anything like that in real life."

Dad steps into the kitchen in time to catch my comment. He cuts his eyes to Mom while adjusting the tie around his neck. They exchange a helpless look, both of them seeming to encourage the other to talk to me. Dad loses the silent battle. When Mom turns away, he picks up the paper and slips it in his briefcase. "Ready, Leanne? I'll drive you to school." Although his hair's been gray since before I was born, lately he's aged in other ways; more crinkles around his eyes when he smiles, a slight grumbling about sore knees, and the addition of bifocal lenses.

I set my bowl in the sink, sling my backpack over my shoulder, and follow him out. He starts the car and we begin our trek through town.

"Should we drive past the construction site?" he asks, pressing on the brake at the end of Chestnut Street. "Would that make you feel better or worse?"

I wrap the strap of my backpack around my hand, squeezing it as though it's a lifeline keeping me from tumbling into a stormy sea. Dad waits for my decision, watching me with a steady warmth in his brown eyes.

I take a deep breath. "I think...I need to see it."

Newly posted signs direct us to the future site of the Saint Piera Holy Shrine. An army of trucks fan out over the field, as trees are cleared and hauled away. Stage one of the construction project has begun. Three photographers and a cluster of elementary school kids stand just beyond the wire fencing, observing the process.

And I suspect, along with the photographers will come more interview requests for me to ignore. Our home phone number is blocked, private, totally inaccessible unless a close friend or family member betrays us. The media contact form on the Leanne Strong website connects to Dad's law office, where his long-time secretary, Celeste, handles requests for publicity materials.

Gazing at the empty field, I feel nothing. Maybe it's because the site doesn't look like a shrine—no crosses or stained glass. Not even a church-like building—not yet.

"Ready to go?" Dad asks.

After we drive away, I mention my thoughts about the media requests to Dad and he smiles. "Celeste forwarded me two emails yesterday. One was from a ghostwriter. Would you be interested in working on a memoir?"

My eyebrows pinch together. "Who writes a memoir when they're still a teenager?"

"The ice skater who won gold at the Olympics last year, a group of teenage YouTubers, the three girls who invented a billion dollar video game—"

"I'm not exactly in their league. Why are you reading teenagers' autobiographies?"

"I might've looked into it for you. So, no memoir. What about a documentary? A graduate film student wants to put together a short film about medical miracles."

"Tell them to talk to Mom. I'm an innocent bystander."

My father clears his throat and I know he's carefully choosing his words. "It's more what you represent, Leanne. People don't necessarily want to know every sordid detail of your backstory. But I think a simple expression of gratitude and some footage of you going about your daily routine would be enough to satisfy the viewing public."

Right. My smiling and waving is enough to make a movie or fill up a book? No way.

"It's too much." My voice cracks. I can't look at him. Like Mom, he tries to hide his disappointment, but...it's there. "You promised never to push me about this. How do I talk about something I don't remember or really understand? What if I say the wrong thing and the Vatican calls?"

"They won't." Dad sounds completely confident, though I have my doubts. "But I'll get back to the writer and the film student, saying you regretfully decline their invitations."

He pulls into the drop-off lane and we coast up to the front entrance of school. Before stepping out of the car, I say, "I wish you could talk to them instead of me. Give them what they want."

"Ah, but it's not me they want, is it?" Dad offers me a small smile. "One day, you'll find the right way to talk about this, Leanne. Only you'll know when."

~

By the last day of school our teachers have run out of creative ways to keep us busy, so we're set free at noon. On their way out, the Girlfriends invite me and Callie to grab lunch before we part ways for the summer. Being a Girlfriend means always being prepared, so of course Mandy Stewert, Katelyn Grant, and Sophia Ling all thought to bring a change of clothes—white denim shorts and flowery tank tops—while

Callie and I bake in our summer uniforms. At least I stowed an extra pair of flip-flops in my locker, which I slide on in place of my knee socks and my incredibly unattractive brown loafers.

By the time Callie slides the Jeep into a parking spot in the center of town, the Girlfriends have already snagged the best table outside of Midnight Pizza, under the striped awning. A car filled with senior guys speeds by and the driver honks, but doesn't stop, much to Katelyn's disappointment.

"We'll just grab something and bring it out," Callie says, eyeing up the Girlfriends' veggie flatbreads.

"Can we please eat junk food?" I ask Callie while the cashier takes a phone order.

She passes her hand over her stomach. "Absolutely. I skipped breakfast and now I'm a bottomless pit with an evil craving for french fries."

We order two slices of pizza and a large basket of fries with a side order of a melted cheese-like substance. When our number's called, we collect our food and head for the outdoor tables.

Callie leans in as we approach the only group eating inside the restaurant. "There's a guy sitting at the table on the left—"

"What? Who?" I crane my neck to check out the person she's talking about. Then I wish I hadn't. Because the guy is Braeden Dalisay, my new neighbor, eating pizza with his mother and a girl with perfectly straight brown hair falling to the middle of her back.

Our eyes meet and hold, but Braeden shows no reaction, happy or sad, at our unexpected reunion. My legs turn to stone and refuse to carry me in any direction—out the door, back to the counter, or closer to Braeden, though a voice in my head begs me to run and hide in the bathroom.

My stellar deer-in-the-headlights impression quickly annoys Callie. "Outside. Let's go." She jabs her elbow into my side.

Tilting my head toward Braeden, I take a cautious step forward. "I know them. I should say hi."

"Hurry up, then. I hate cold fries," Callie says before making her escape.

Left alone with the Dalisays, I wonder if I should reintroduce myself. Will they recognize me outside the bubble of Chestnut Street? Mrs. Dalisay looks up the instant I decide to chicken out and head for the exit. She raises her arm and waves it back in forth like a windshield wiper, making it impossible for me to pretend I don't see her.

"Leanne! I was just talking about you."

At the sound of his mom's voice, Braeden leans across the table, lifting a slice of pizza with cheese dripping over the sides.

"The miracle girl?" The girl's dark hair swings over her shoulder when she shoots to her feet. She aims a wide-eyed stare my way, looking like she's expecting me to summon a hurricane.

"Sami, this is Leanne Strong, our new neighbor," Mrs. Dalisay says, resting her hand on her daughter's shoulder.

Behind Sami, Braeden coughs, pushing my attention away from his sister. Tension hums in the air and I sense an unspoken warning—he knows I'm about to crush his sister with my total lack of miraculous behavior.

I juggle my fries and drink around and extend a hand. "Hi, Sami. Welcome to Spring River."

She shakes my hand, peering up at me with stars in her big brown eyes. "Are you the real Leanne Strong?"

"Um, I'm not sure if there's another one of me, but as far

as I know I'm real."

"No, it's definitely you. You're much older than the picture on your website, though."

I wonder what constitutes much – three years, five, or fifteen. Before I think too hard about it, Sami continues, "I asked Braeden to introduce us, but he's always busy. I thought maybe touching you would bring me good luck." She lifts her hand again and brushes her fingers over my bare arm. My muscles tense as I fight the urge to flinch.

"Did she zing some miracle juice into you, Samster?" Braeden asks, in a dry voice.

Sami holds her fingers in front of her face. "I don't feel different, but it was worth a try. Maybe you can stop by some time?" She lowers her hand and locks her eyes with mine, pleading. "I don't have any friends."

"Sami! That's not true at all." Mrs. Dalisay looks shocked. "You keep in touch with the girls from your old school. And Gabby."

"I meant friends in Spring River." Sami scrunches her face. "None of the girls from Eddytown want to take two buses and walk four miles to hang out with me. And Gabby's not exactly my friend. She's just someone I know from camp."

Braeden coughs again, which I interpret as his unspoken agreement.

"Dad promised to drive you back to Eddytown whenever you want," Mrs. Dalisay says.

"When he's not working, which is never." Sami huffs loudly before she seems to remember this argument wasn't the point of the conversation. "Anyway, if my old friends decide to visit, I'm sure they'd love to meet you, Leanne."

"Sorry, I meant to stop by, but with school ending and

everything..." My words trail off into an uncomfortable silence.

"Oh, it's fine," Sami says. "Your hair is pretty. Emeline would've loved it."

Braeden and his mom exchange a wide-eyed look and I sense I'm missing something important.

"Emeline? Your friend from Eddytown?"

"No," Sami says, with a frown. "My sister. She died last year. That's why we moved to Spring River. Mom thought we needed a fresh start."

My chest burns, like a spark flew out of the pizza oven and lit a fire inside my pounding heart. "I—I'm sorry," I whisper. It's all I can think to say.

"Thank you, Leanne. We should have told you and your mother about Emeline the other day," Mrs. Dalisay cuts in. Her face is pale. "It's just—"

"Not something we bring up the first time we meet people," Braeden says in a flat tone. "Back home, everyone knew about her."

A greasy pizza smell wafts in the air, raising a coil of nausea in my stomach. I might be sick. But I can't just run out of here, like I don't care.

Turning back to Sami, I ask, "Where will you go to school next year?"

"I'm starting at Holy Family." She flashes a small smile. "That's where you go, right? We were supposed to take a tour yesterday, but with all the news cameras in the parking lot, the principal asked if we could reschedule. Maybe you could show me around?"

"Sure. Anytime." I allow a breath to escape from my tight chest and move toward the exit. "And I think my mom wants to invite you all over for dinner."

"We'd love to," Mrs. Dalisay answers immediately.

I press my arm to the door, ready to leave, though the conversation feels unfinished. Should I ask more questions about Emeline? Is there an acceptable way to talk about death in the middle of a pizzeria? I pause, not wanting to abandon the Dalisays, but unsure of what to say to them. The full impact of Sami's words hits me and I feel worse than ever about my June eighth tantrum. Who complains about a miracle in front of a family suffering from the worst kind of loss? Only a selfish, entitled, spoiled brat. A girl so far removed from pain and suffering that she fails to pick up on someone else's sadness, even when it's so carefully laid out in front of her.

"I-I have to go. My friends are waiting."

But the Dalisays have already moved on. Glancing back once more, I catch Braeden placing the last slice of pizza on his sister's plate while Mrs. Dalisay watches them with a sad half-smile.

~

Outside, the end of school celebrations continue. My pulse hammers as I make my way through the growing crowd, desperate to find Callie. I wind up walking right past her, still replaying the conversation with the Dalisays in my head. She breaks away from the girls and tugs my sleeve, pulling me toward an empty table on the edge of the busy social scene.

"How do you know Braeden Dalisay?"

My flip-flop catches in the uneven pavement. I shake my toe loose and stop myself from falling. "He's my new neighbor. How do you know him?"

"I was trying to tell you about it when we were inside, but you said you already knew him. He's a baseball phenom.

Don't you follow the local sports updates on Twitter or Insta?"

"I'm not on social media," I remind her. We find an empty bench, behind the crowded tables. I prop the basket of fries on my lap. "And club tennis doesn't get much coverage in the local papers. You're the varsity athlete, not me."

Callie's eyes cut toward the pizzeria. "True, but right now he's looking at *you* through the window, not me. And when we were waiting for our food, he was checking you out." She reaches for a fry. "I notice these things."

"He probably thought he recognized me but couldn't remember where we'd met."

"He definitely knows you. You're the most famous high school student in Pennsylvania. And he's the *second* most famous high school student in Pennsylvania. It's a wonder you haven't met before now. Don't you have famous people conventions to attend in your spare time?"

I sink my teeth into a slice and feel hot cheese scorch the top of my mouth. "He's famous? Because of baseball?" Reaching for my cup, I sip ice water to numb the burning pain.

"From what I hear, he's already made a verbal commitment to State U. He throws an eighty-mile-an-hour fastball."

"Is that good?"

Callie laughs. "Considering you probably can't throw over thirty, yes."

I take another long sip of water. "His family moved into the Murrays' old place."

"Awesome. We'll hang out at your house this summer and invite him over. Are you sharing those fries or what?" Callie grabs a handful and sneaks another glance toward the window. "Why did he move to Spring River? He's an all-star in his old school district."

"He had a sister, Emeline...she, um...died."

Callie freezes, french fry dangling from her hand. "Oh, wow. That's just...awful."

When I risk a glimpse through the pizzeria window, Sami's not looking, but my eyes meet Braeden's again. I look away first. "Since he's already locked up a scholarship, his senior year doesn't really matter, does it?"

"Apparently not. Anyway, if Braeden Dalisay shows up at Holy Family next year, he'll be instantly popular. I wonder how Katelyn's groupmissed him."

"They probably didn't bother looking in his direction. He was sitting with his sister and his mom. Here, I'm not hungry. Finish the fries."

When I pass her the basket, she cradles it against her like she's holding a newborn. "Miracle cures and an awesome neighbor. You really are a lucky girl, aren't you?"

"Not quite. I'm pretty sure he hates me." I fill Callie in on my after-school, June eighth outburst.

She winces. "Ouch. He heard you complain? And then you find out his sister died."

"Right. So, no, he's not interested. If he ever was, he definitely isn't now."

But Callie refuses to let it go. "Maybe your first impression wasn't the greatest. It doesn't mean—"

"Cal, stop. I'm not interested in him either. The no-dating rule, remember?"

"Come on, Leanne. For Braeden Dalisay, you can make an exception."

"No exceptions. I'll date in college, after I change my name and dye my hair. I want to meet guys who don't know my history before they ask me out."

Another car filled with seniors drives by, blasting the radio. Someone tosses a Frisbee out of the window. It lands at Callie's feet and she kicks it away. "So, if you're not interested, can I talk to him?"

"Of course you can talk to him." But my teeth grind together as I chew my bite of pizza. I'm not sure why I would care if Callie dated Braeden, but the idea doesn't sit right with me. Still, she's my best friend and deserves my support. "You're both super-athletes. You can be a power couple at Holy Family next year."

Chapter 5

For the rest of the week, I go out of my way to avoid Braeden and Sami Dalisay. And it's not that I don't feel guilty about my behavior, because I really do. But the way Sami looked at me, the way she touched me...she wants something I can't give her. And seeing Braeden again made me uncomfortable for reasons I can't begin to explain.

Sami's probably sitting in her house, across the street, waiting for a big story about my miracle. Like angels floated down from the heavens and trumpets blared. A voice spoke to me and told me I was healed. Go and spread the good word to all men, women, and children. And so forth.

But I've got nothing.

I'm not sure how other miracles happen, but mine was a quiet one. From what I've been told, the earth didn't shake. The sun didn't slide out of focus. When I picture that night, I imagine my mother tucking me into my crib and kissing me goodnight. Maybe I'd had a bad day and a tear dropped from her eye onto my cheek. Up in heaven, a holy woman noticed that one tear. She saw it wash over me. She felt my pain and

Mom's pain. Dad's pain, too, although Dad was in the middle of his angry phase, according to Mom. He worked off his frustration by single-handedly taking on the judicial system of Spring River County and arguing with every insurance company who dared to question or deny payment for my medical care.

So, after observing the mess below, Saint Piera asked someone for help. Did she go directly to God? Or are there other official channels for miracle-granting? Was it a long process or just a short exchange of prayer and emotion? To be honest, I have a hard time picturing how that part of it worked.

And when the miracle occurred, did I feel the warmth of a heavenly embrace? Did my crying stop when the pain suddenly lifted? I wish I could remember. If someone besides me had witnessed the miracle, my parents might have avoided five years of court appearances, dealing with skeptical doctors and papal authorities as they worked through the process of documenting my certifiable, beyond a doubt unalterable medical condition which was cured without a possible scientific explanation.

According to the transcripts, even Dr. Wagner, the lone dissenter among the expert medical panel, admitted that sometimes things happen which cannot be explained by existing medical knowledge. Still, he said my cure could not be the result of a miracle—because, according to his testimony, I fell into a gray area. His extremely technical term was "a fluke." When my father questioned the expert panel, Dr. Wagner suggested I might have been improperly diagnosed from the start. Possibly, whatever was wrong with my spine clicked into the correct position after a growth spurt. Just clicked. Overnight.

Or maybe, my father responded, the healing power of

prayer is a true phenomenon.

Something we'll never be able to explain, but we accept as our truth.

~

My bedroom window overlooks the Dalisays' front yard. I glance at their house every so often, watching Braeden come and go in his small black car with headlights shaped like bug eyes. When he's home, he spends hours outside, hurling balls against a person-sized net that bounces his throw back into his glove. The rhythm of his pitches melts into the background noise of Chestnut Street. If he misses a day, or even a few hours, I start to wonder about him.

Sunday night, after the sun sinks behind the trees, Mrs. Dalisay and Sami walk up and down our tree-lined street. Sami ties a sweatshirt around her waist, despite the blast of early summer heat gripping the atmosphere with a choking hold. They pause in front of my house and Sami lifts her eyes to my bedroom window. Guilt slices through me as I tug the shade down.

I need to stop hiding and keep my promise to visit. But for some reason, I have trouble taking the first step across the street.

~

For my first day of work, I wear a flowered skirt and yellow top. Dad insists on professional dress in the office, though his walk-in clients are few and far between. Hoping he doesn't mind casual footwear, I slide on my flip flops, nice ones with silk flowers sewn on the straps.

Golden sunlight washes over the sidewalk, adding a gentle warmth to the air before the day takes a turn into oppressive heat. The court house sits in the center of town, with streets flung out from the sprawling red brick building like spokes on a wheel. Dad's law office is a converted mint-green Victorian overlooking one of the busier side streets. A wooden shingle hangs by the front door, reading "Jason Strong, Attorney at Law." Mom painted the sign when he opened his own practice and she touches up the black lettering every year.

A musty smell lingers in the entryway, though Dad keeps the windows cracked open whenever he's in the office. The chatter of a morning talk show penetrates the thin walls, drifting out of the small café next door. Dad set up shop on the second floor because it's the nicer half of the building, but not by much. Downstairs, he stores old files, an outdated law library, and a bunch of Leanne Strong media kits.

In the dark waiting area, I yank the pull string to open the blinds, flooding the room with light. Celeste hasn't arrived but someone turned on the coffee machine, releasing a rich scent of hazelnut.

Farther down the hallway, Dad's office door hangs open. I ditch my lunch bag in the mini-fridge before poking my head in.

"Reporting for duty. Where should I start?"

"Hi, honey." Dad stands and holds out his fist. We knock hands.

"No terms of endearment at work. And what's with the fist bump? Trying to up your cool factor?" I think of Callie's assurance that no dad is exciting. My parents' existence never bothers me much, possibly due to my state of only-childness. They're all I've ever had as far as in-house entertainment.

"Hey, I've been cool longer than you've been alive," he says, looking highly offended.

I laugh. "Whatever, dude."

Dad runs a finger down a hand-written list of to-dos. "Can

you take care of the closed case files in the conference room? Pack them in boxes and label them for storage."

"I'm on it. And I have some new ideas about your filing system." I rest my hip against the doorframe. "You need to at least try to go paperless."

He picks up his yellow pad and clutches it against his chest. "But I like paper."

I hold out my hand and step forward slowly, ready to stage an intervention. "You can do it, Dad. Cool people use scanners. There's even an app on your phone to take a picture, turn it into a pdf and send the file into your email."

"Huh?" He appears mystified.

"An app, Dad. You know what that is, right?"

Heaving a dramatic sigh, he sets the pad back on the desk. "For you, I'll try. But good luck turning Celeste over to the dark side when she gets back from vacation."

"No Celeste?" Darn. I was looking forward to catching up with her and easing back into work.

Dad shakes his head. "Family trip to Florida."

"She's away all week?" The gears in my mind begin to turn. "Maybe I can make a few tiny changes while she's away. When she gets back, she'll have no choice but to adapt."

Excited to start my new project, I spring out of Dad's office. Throwing open the door to the conference room, I nearly collide with someone carrying a triple stack of storage boxes.

"Sorry, I didn't see—" My apology dies in mid-air when Braeden Dalisay peers out from behind the boxes.

"Hey, Leanne." His dark eyes mirror my surprise. Lifting the stack higher, he turns sideways to let me pass. My mouth hangs open and I can't gain enough control over my facial muscles to snap it closed. Pulse racing, I grab a stray case file from the long table before circling back to Dad, stopping in front of his desk.

"Finished already, sweetheart?" Dad glances up from his newspaper. "Sit down and we'll go over our game plan for the rest of the week."

"Why is he here?" I ask, remaining upright.

"By *he*, I assume you mean Braeden." Dad flips to the business page. "Patti Dalisay asked Mom if she knew of anyone hiring for the summer. With all the work I've picked up lately, I told her I could use an extra hand around the office."

"Why didn't you tell me about it?"

"Did you need to know before right now?"

"Yes, I really did. I'm sorry, Dad, but I can't work with him," I say, striving for total honesty. "He hates me."

Dad drags his eyes away from the headlines. "What makes you think that?" he asks in his calm, perfectly rational, lawyer voice.

"Did Mom tell you about what I said in front of him and Mrs. Dalisay? About not wanting to be part of the shrine dedication?"

"You said that? Out loud? In front of other people?" Dad moves from simply confused to totally lost. Usually I do carry some semblance of politeness.

"On June eighth. I was in Sister Bernadette's office when I saw Monsignor on TV, talking about how I'd agreed to make a public appearance. But no one bothered to tell me about it before his big announcement. After school, I walked in the house and...made my feelings about the matter known." I pause to catch my breath. "I didn't know *he* was listening."

"I'm sure *he* didn't hear you," Dad insists.

I bite back a snap of laughter. "I was loud, Dad. Very loud." I drop my voice to a whisper. "And then, I found out his sister, um..."

"Yes, I know about Emeline." Dad sinks back in his chair. "Patti told Mom."

"So...you understand my situation, right?" I give Dad a few seconds to connect the dots. He flips out his palm, meaning he doesn't. "Think about it, Dad. What would you think if a girl who was granted this awesome miracle stomped in the house and complained about it? Wouldn't you want to run away from her as fast as possible? Especially after your your own sister..." I let the words trail off.

"Not necessarily." He raises a finger in the air, ready to state his case, when we're interrupted by a knock at the door. I back up and yank it open.

Braeden stands there, blinking at the force of my movement. "Mr. Strong? I've finished moving those boxes. What can I do next?"

Gag. He's already kissing up. And he's making me look like a total slacker.

Dad shoots me a look which I interpret as him saying play nice. "Leanne, why don't you show our newest employee how to log into the network? Since you want to turn this place into the paperless office of the future." He cracks a vengeful smile. "The two of you can enter the latest case updates and scan the hardcopies in Celeste's inbox."

"Yes, sir," Braeden says before darting away. I raise my eyes to the ceiling, muttering a quick appeal for divine intervention. When none is forthcoming, I blow out a breath and huff my way out of my father's office.

In the hallway, Braeden waits for me to catch up, standing perfectly straight, with his arms at his side, like one of the marble statues in the mock-ups of the Saint Piera shrine. His dark eyebrows knit together while he studies me carefully, like he's unsure if I'm here to help him or make his life more difficult. I wish I'd taken Callie up on her offer to recommend me for a camp counselor job.

"We're going this way." I swing past Braeden into the reception area. He follows at a distance, then stands back and watches me fight with the lever on Celeste's chair as I adjust the height to a comfortable position. When I punch the start button on her ancient laptop, the processor hums and vibrates, like it's ten seconds away from going up in smoke.

"Pull up a chair." I gesture to the empty spot behind the front desk. He lifts one of the folded chairs in the waiting area over the desk and sets it next to mine. I swallow my reaction, but, truly, it's hard not to be impressed by the way he swings furniture around like he's picking up a handful of toothpicks.

We stare at the screen, pretending to be fascinated by the flickering cursor. What should I say to him? Should I congratulate him on his new job? I want to apologize for my horrible remarks on June eighth, but dragging up the episode again seems like a bad idea. Especially if Dad's right and Braeden has forgotten about it. Yet somehow, I suspect he remembers every ungrateful word I said.

"You should come over and hang out with Sami." Braeden stretches his long legs under the desk as the computer clicks and beeps. The screen flickers, first black and then blue. "She keeps asking about you."

My shoulders elevate. "I'll try to stop by," I manage, though my mouth suddenly goes dry.

He shifts in his seat and flexes his arm at the elbow. "Is it always so quiet in here?"

I offer him a tight grin. "You haven't met Celeste. She talks a lot. And Mia, Dad's paralegal, is chatty too. Sometimes clients come in, but I don't really deal with them. You know, the whole confidentiality thing..."

"Gotcha. Wouldn't want to accidentally reveal any nasty secrets," Braeden agrees.

"Yeah, something like that. But overall this place is pretty dull," I say, wondering if I can convince him to quit without being too obvious about it. When I left for work this morning, I had certain expectations about my summer job. With a new person in the office, my whole routine will be thrown off. Mia, Celeste and I won't be able to chat about fun stuff while Dad's in court. I'll need to set an example and be on my best behavior every minute of the day. "Dad mostly writes wills and reviews contracts. Occasionally he takes on a lawsuit. Divorces, broken contracts, landlords versus tenants. Some of them can get ugly."

"Like fist fights?" Braeden perks up at the idea.

"No," I quickly correct him. "Just a bunch of yelling and people storming out of the conference room. Dad warns me ahead of time to stay in the file room when the disgruntled people come in."

Braeden's phone pings. He removes it from his pocket and fires off a quick text. "I'm surprised a girl like you even works. I thought you'd be off greeting fans at paid appearances. Signing autographs." Although his words could be interpreted as simple curiosity, something in the tone of his voice stirs up a hornets' nest in my stomach. I bite back a flicker of irritation. Does he really think anyone would pay to hear me talk about nothing? As if.

My fingers brush over my Saint Piera medal, dangling at the end of its thin chain. It was a gift from the Sisters of Saint Piera, given to me at the canonization. "I'm not what you think."

"True," Braeden says. "You're not anything like I

thought."

The computer screen blinks twice and the login prompt appears.

"Oh, look! Success," I say. "Do you know how to work a scanner?"

He looks at me like I've asked if he understands English. "That's kind of basic, isn't it?"

"For me, yes. But no one else in this office seems to understand twenty-first century technology. Mia has a clunker of a PC and Dad still writes notes on a legal pad. This summer, I was hoping to eliminate some of the piles." I gesture to the rolling hills and mountains of paper on Celeste's desk.

Braeden's eyes brighten and he sits up straighter in his chair, looking at me like I just discovered plutonium. "Did you know I wrote an entire term paper on paper recycling?"

My eyes widen. "No way. How would I know that?"

"Twenty pages about how to reduce paper and increase our recycling rate. Handed it to my teacher on a flash drive, and then—guess what?"

"She made you print it out, anyway?"

His mouth twitches into a fast smile. For a heartbeat, the awkwardness between us slips away.

"You and I are on a mission this summer." Braeden taps the pile of legal documents closest to him. "All of this will be gone before we leave."

I sink my chin into my hand. "I was hoping for a twenty-five percent reduction. But I could hide the printer toner to force change."

Braeden nods. "Force change. I like it."

"Are you kiddos ganging up on me already?" Dad's voice floats out of his office.

"No, not at all, sir," Braeden calls back and I raise my hand to my mouth, preventing my laughter from slipping out.

Maybe he is worth keeping around, if only for entertainment purposes.

Chapter 6

Braeden and Sami are playing catch in their front yard. She's wearing a helmet, kneeling on the grass, holding up a glove. The thwack of the ball isn't nearly as loud as when he throws against the net on their driveway. They speak to each other using nicknames and incomplete sentences, a secret brother-sister language, one I've never learned as an only child. Watching them together, I wonder if I've missed out on something. Something important.

Since that first day in the office, Braeden pretty much ignores me. He seems to have forgotten about our war against paper. We spend hours avoiding each other without making it obvious. He takes up space in the conference room, which means I'm stuck at the front desk, answering phones in Celeste's absence.

At lunch, I eat a salad at the small table set up in the file room, though it means missing my favorite break-time activity—watching the streams of lawyers, shoppers, and kids passing on the street below. The excitement of returning to my summer job fades and the work becomes tedious. I sneak in some time with the scanner, eliminating half of Celeste's inbox, but Braeden's presence puts a huge dent in my motivation. If we're competing for the best office assistant award, he can have the title. I'm only here to help Dad and collect my paycheck.

When Mia finally returns after a string of research days in the law library, I'm sitting at Celeste's desk, sorting through mail and checking e-mails. Mia is a cat person and her love of felines bleeds into her wardrobe. Today, she's wearing a white linen dress with a gray leopard-print jacket. She's also sporting a new, layered haircut and the curled ends of her long brown hair bounce from her shoulders as she approaches the front desk.

"Ready for another fun summer, Leanne?"

"Always. What's new, Mia?"

She picks up the mail I dropped in her inbox and starts to fill me in on her recent trip to the beach when Braeden barges out of the file room, always in a hurry for no apparent reason. Mia's eyes widen. After he flies by, she leans over the front desk.

"Who is that?"

I scribble a number on a notepad, assuming Dad still hasn't figured out how to use the digital messaging service to check his voicemail. He's kind of clueless about anything falling under Celeste's job definition. "That's our summer intern, Braeden."

"He's, um, quite unexpected," she says, sounding not very future-lawyerly. "How old is he?"

I rip the message sheet from the pad. "Around seventeen or eighteen, I think."

Mia counts out their age difference, holding up six fingers. "Oh, darn. He looks older, don't you think?"

"Maybe. He's very...tall." I shove an old draft of a legal brief through the shredder. "Don't you have a boyfriend?"

"We broke up last month." She buffs her nails on her jacket. "He was too serious. And always tired after work. We spent two weeks sitting on the sofa and binge watching sci-fi, then I called it quits." She darts her eyes toward the open conference room door. "What do you think of the new guy?"

"He's okay, so far." I withhold any further opinion on the matter. I'm beginning to think my view of Braeden might be tainted.

On her way to her office, Mia knocks on the open conference room door. "Welcome, Braeden. I'm Mia Jang, Jason's paralegal," she says in a super-cheery voice.

Needless to say, Braeden's interest in a future legal career (after a potential baseball career) results in an insta-friendship between him and Mia. Over lunch, she goes out of her way to explain the latest changes in court procedures to him. The clear, monotone voice she uses when she's trying to appear professional projects out of her office, straight up to the waiting area. I hear everything, including when she invites him to a hangout with her law school friends. He thanks her, saying he has a baseball game and can't make it.

Braeden and Mia seem to have clicked, leaving me in the role of a third wheel, which lessens the pressure I feel working around him. Because if Braeden talks to Mia, he won't talk to me. And not talking to Braeden means not talking about the reason why I'm avoiding his sister. Which makes me feel less guilty about being a bad neighbor.

~

After a week of containment in Dad's office, I need to breathe fresh air, despite the pressing heat. Friday night, my parents leave for dinner with friends. The house is too quiet. I text Callie about catching a movie, but she responds back saying she's on her way to the beach with her parents. When clouds move in and cover the setting sun, I haul one of my summer reading assignments out to the back patio and light a lemon-scented candle to keep the bugs away.

At the end of chapter two, the doorbell rings, sparking an uneasy tremor in my chest. My parents still remind me not to open the door every time they leave the house, though I wouldn't let strangers inside, even if they gave me permission. But tonight when I glance at the security monitor hooked up to a camera above our front door, I see Sami, smiling and waving.

"Oh, good, you're here," she says when I crack open the door. "Braeden said you might be out on a date."

"No, not tonight," I say. Or any night, really. Why would he say that?

Closer to the sidewalk, a skinny girl with yellow-blond hair paces up and down the driveway. She tugs at the waist of her baggy jeans, then pulls on the hem of her faded purple T-shirt.

Sami waves the girl closer. "Gabby wants to meet you." The three of us stare at each other as a hidden cricket launches into a chirping song. Sami shifts her weight back and forth nervously, pulling at a lock of her long hair, dark brown like her brother's, but with more of a reddish tint.

Her eyes slide to her friend and I get the sense that Sami wants me to do or say something to impress Gabby. It's not a new feeling for me. Unfortunately, I'm never sure exactly how to accomplish this. Wearing flip-flops, ratty jean shorts and an old tank top, I'm not super-impressive looking.

After I wave to Gabby, Sami turns back to me. "I like your

necklace."

I run my thumb over the silver medal, engraved with the likeness of Saint Piera, her arms extended over a kneeling girl. "Thanks. It was a gift from the Sisters of Saint Piera." Unsure what to say next, I adjust my headband to capture a loose lock of hair.

Gabby pulls her phone from her pocket and swipes her hand over the screen.

Sami ignores her friend and steps closer to me. "What are you reading?"

I hold up the book in my hand. "American short stories. I need to pick one to write about for AP English. I'd rather read a fantasy novel or something written in this century, though."

Sami grins. "Me too. What's your favorite book, Gabby?"

Snapping her eyes from her phone, Gabby frowns. "I don't read much. I play drums, remember?"

Sami's mouth opens and closes. "Oh. Right." After the briefest hesitation, she continues. "Gabby plays in a band. She loves music."

"What type of music?" I ask.

"Everything. Classic rock, pop, jazz, folk. We're working on a song of our own, too. I co-wrote it with a friend." Gabby's lips curl into a smile, but her blue eyes don't appear to match the warmth of her expression.

"I met Gabby in bereavement camp last summer. Her dad died the week after my sister," Sami blurts out.

Gabby's cheeks turn pink. "Do you have to tell everyone, Sami?"

"I'm sorry, but I just thought...sometimes it's hard to say the words out loud...and you might want Leanne to know about it."

"It's nice that the two of you kept in touch," I whisper,

reluctant to intrude in their discussion.

Sami shoots me a grateful smile. "Yeah. It was a really great camp. We're trying to decide if we want to go back this year."

Gabby drops her phone into her pocket. "Sami and I were bunkmates. But this summer I'm busy with my band." Looking at me, her eyes narrow. "I like your hair. How did you do the small braid in the front?"

"I followed a YouTube tutorial." I lift my hand to my hair and smooth back a loose piece. "I'm practicing some new styles. Can I try one out on you?"

At my offer, Gabby's eyes brighten. "Will I look like Katniss Everdeen?"

"A side braid? That one took me months to perfect." Standing behind her, on the highest step, I wind together sections of her fine, blond hair. When I've tucked every last piece into the slanted braid, I roll the ever-present elastic band off my wrist and secure the loose ends.

"Not bad," Sami says, leaning closer to examine my work. "Want to practice on me?"

I run my hands over Sami's thick waves, judging the texture. "Can I try a fishtail?"

"Can you do a double?"

It takes a few attempts to work all of Sami's hair into twin fishtails, but the end result is adorable. I snap a quick phone photo for her. "It's easier to practice on someone else. I never pull the fishtail tight enough when I try it on myself."

"This is perfect. My hair's too long for summer." She shakes her head, swinging the twin braids. "I used to chop six inches off every year. But Mom hasn't found a hairdresser in Spring River. The shop we went to back home...they all knew Em."

"I can try, if you want a blunt cut. I can't do layers."

"Really?" Sami looks impressed.

"My aunt's a hair dresser. She taught me a few of her tricks."

"Can you add purple streaks, too?"

I bite back a laugh. "Would your mom be okay with it?"

"Probably not." Sami sighs. "Those fun colors work better on light hair, anyway."

"Let Leanne try," Gabby says. "You might be surprised."

"Maybe a temporary color to start, or hair chalk," I say, trying to brainstorm. "So, how do you like your new house, Sami?"

She turns her eyes toward her home, studying the white siding and black shutters as though she's seeing them for the first time. "It's smaller than our old house. But Mom says with Braeden going to State U next year, we won't need as much room."

"His scholarship is already locked up, then?"

"Pretty much. Unless he fails senior year, but he won't. He's an undercover nerd, posing as a cool baseball player."

We share a smile before I say, "Anyone who enjoys working in a law office definitely has some nerd potential."

As if he can hear us talking about him, Braeden suddenly appears, striding across the street. He's wearing his baseball uniform and I remember him telling Mia about his game tonight.

"C'mon, Samster. Mom's looking for you and I gotta be at the field in ten minutes."

"They're fine here, if they want to stay," I say, trying hard not to notice the way his uniform shirt hugs his chest.

Sami shoos him away. "Go to your game, Braeden, and leave us alone. Tell Mom I'm hanging out with Leanne."

"Yup, looks like a real party going on here." Braeden's dark eyes are lit with amusement as his gaze sweeps over the three of us before resting on me. "If you're sure, Leanne."

"We're having fun," I insist. "Have a good game. Get a hit or strike someone out, or whatever."

His mouth twitches into a smile. "Whatever." With a nod of his head, he retreats. A minute later we hear his car roar to life and drive away.

"Pull up a chair, girls. This my version of an exciting Friday night." I motion to the wicker furniture sitting on the porch. As darkness takes over and the wind picks up enough to toss the occasional loose paper along the sidewalk, we drop all talk of bereavement and miracles. Sami and Gabby seem happy to have someone listen to them go on about boys, books, and music. Sami barrages me with questions about the freshman teachers at Holy Family. I'm reciting a list of my favorite science classes when a bolt of lightning flames down from the sky, landing somewhere in the woods behind our neighborhood. The impact shakes the entire block.

Screaming, the girls shoot to their feet.

"We need to leave. Right now," Sami says, her voice shaking.

The sky breaks open and heavy raindrops begin to fall.

"Wait. Take an umbrella." I run inside and dig out a pair from the closet. A clap of thunder triggers a surge of adrenaline shooting through my chest.

I rush back outside, push up one umbrella and hand it to Gabby. "Let me walk you home."

Sami doesn't object when I throw my arm around her shoulders to keep her under the cover of the second umbrella as we sprint across the street. Wind-swept rain stings my bare legs. When I trip over the curb, she lets out a surprised squeak.

I force out a fake laugh to keep her calm. We pick up speed

as a strong gust turns the umbrella inside out and throws rain in my face. Sami grabs my arm and drags me across the lawn. Thunder booms again and she darts ahead while I toss my sweatshirt over my head, letting the rain slide from my hair onto my face.

We make it to the safety of the Dalisays' driveway just as Braeden returns. He jumps out of his car and punches a code in the security pad next to the garage to open the door. Standing under cover, the four of us watch Chestnut Street turn into a river.

Braeden hangs his cap on a hook and uses his forearm to push the front of his wet hair higher, off his forehead. "Storm's headed in from the west. Hit the ball field first and the game was called." Lightning pops like a camera flash, illuminating his face. "You girls okay?"

"Fine," Sami says, but her voice trembles.

"Sami's petrified of lightning," Braeden says.

Gabby releases a burst of laughter.

Sami glares at her brother. "Shut up, Braeden."

Gabby spreads her arms wide and steps out of the garage. Thunder crashes above her and she answers it with a roar. "Rain, rain go away."

"Gabby, come back inside," Sami screams, revealing her true terror level.

I place my hand on her shoulder and squeeze. "Look, the lightning's moved away." I point at the sky, showing her the flashes of white off in the distance. Still, I wonder if it's safe enough for me to run back home. It's raining so hard I can't even see my porch light right now.

"If you want to wait it out, come inside with us," Braeden says, startling me from my thoughts.

I hesitate. "Thanks, but I left my phone at home. My parents might worry if they call in the middle of a storm and I don't answer."

He reaches for a blue and white golf umbrella. "Take this. It'll hold up against the wind better than your small one."

He snaps it open and hands it to me. I tuck my smaller umbrellas under my arm and take off, calling goodbye to the three of them over the howling wind.

Chapter 7

"Leanne, we're late," Dad calls up the stairs. I slide three long bobby pins in the front of my hair to pull the heaviest pieces away from my face. Intending to fix my makeup in the car, I drop eyeshadow and lip gloss in my purse, half-wondering why I'm making such an effort for church this morning. I suppose it's the miracle factor. Since the shrine announcement, I feel more attention on me, especially in the religious world.

Mom, Dad and I take our usual seats right as Monsignor marches up the aisle. Not many people choose to sit up front, but the large buffer of empty pews surrounding us helps take some of the pressure off; I swear Mom and Dad would sit on the altar if Monsignor invited them. But, from this part of the church, if anyone is staring at me, they're looking at the back of my head and chances are they won't notice my less-than-perfect attention span.

Toward the end of the opening prayers, the side doors swing open and the Dalisay family appears. Braeden and Sami trail behind their parents, and the four of them make a beeline for the pew in front of us. Even though Monsignor's in the middle of welcoming everyone to church on this fine summer morning, Dad extends his hand to shake Mr. Dalisay's and they exchange a quiet introduction. Braeden and Sami's dad has dark hair, thinner in front, and he's wearing round glasses, but still, he's easily imaginable as the future version of Braeden.

Quiet murmurs roll through the church when the regulars notice the Dalisays. In Spring River, new families always spark an interest. Monsignor steps up to the pulpit to address the crowd and we settle in for the long haul. The cooling system at St. Genevieve's dips to ice box levels in the summer, prompting goose bumps to pop up on my arms, under my thin sweater.

After some shuffling around, Braeden winds up sitting in front of me and I spend most of my time staring at the back of his unruly dark hair. He's extremely adept at stillness; the guy barely moves as Monsignor talks about today's readings, while I fold and unfold my hands and bounce my knee as my mind wanders. Thankfully, Mom and Dad are long past quizzing me over Sunday dinner. I failed their church tests enough times to raise their annoyance, but still get decent grades in theology class.

When the time comes to exchange a greeting with those around us, I hold back, letting the Dalisay siblings make the first move. Sami digs her elbow into Braeden's side. He grabs her hand, pumping hard until she's fighting laughter. Watching them, I smile, and when he directs his attention my way, his eyes catch mine.

"Psst. Leanne." Sami leans over the pew, clasping my fingers in hers before I decide what to do about her brother. When she turns away, Braeden extends his hand. After a pause, I return the gesture. He curls his fingers slightly, pressing his thumb over mine, keeping his touch light. Our eyes are locked, tighter than his strong grip and I feel like whatever's happening between us isn't meant to be a church-related activity. Dad must agree, because he shifts closer and clears his throat, signaling it's time to move on with the process. I drop my hand, Braeden turns away, and mass continues. But my fingers remained curled into a fist, like I'm reluctant to lose the sensation of his touch in the palm of my hand.

"We never scheduled your welcome to the neighborhood dinner," Mom says to Mrs. Dalisay after introducing our new neighbors to Monsignor and stopping to talk to about ten other church friends on our way out.

Oh, no. Not today. Please. My thumb brushes over my Saint Piera medal, turning my thoughts into an unspoken prayer.

"Are you free this afternoon?" Mom asks.

Say no. Say no. Say no.

"What time? Can I bring dessert or salad?" Mrs. Dalisay makes arrangements without consulting the rest of her family.

Braeden's shadow hits the sidewalk in front of me. "Looks like we're spending the day together."

I step to the side and slow my pace, allowing him to catch up. "If the moms have anything to say about it, I guess we are."

"That could be hard for you." He shoves his hands in his pockets. "I mean, how will you ignore me when we're sitting at the same table?"

My mouth falls open. Am I so blatantly obvious? It's not

like he's Mister Overly-Friendly. "Hey, you can't—" But, before I toss an accusation back at him, he disappears into his family's minivan.

~

I change out of my church clothes, balling up my sweater and tossing it on the bed. If Braeden wants me to talk to him, then fine. I have no problem with polite conversation. In fact, I'll prove how nice I can be. Stun him with my friendliness.

At least his sister likes me. Wait. Does she? I'm not a hundred percent sure about that, either.

Before Mom calls me to help with dinner, I check in with Callie. She picks up her phone on the fourth ring.

"Sorry to interrupt your vacation," I say.

"What? Oh, we came home," Callie says. "My parents started arguing again. Dad said the hotel Mom picked was too expensive and Mom said stop worrying about money, we should just enjoy being together. So Dad said let's enjoy being together at home. After we checked out, I called work and my boss said I can start early."

"That's good, right?" I ask, hoping to cheer her up. "Because, cute guys. And you can make more money to pay for our movie nights."

Her laugh carries a trace of bitterness. "Sure. It's the ultimate in coolness. Never thought I'd prefer work to the beach, but you know how it goes."

I truly don't. Most of the time, my parents have a pretty solid, uneventful relationship.

"Speaking of movies, want to catch the late show? *Today or Tomorrow* opened this weekend," she says after a pause.

Today or Tomorrow ranks high on our summer watch list with its current one-point-five star ranking on our favorite movie fan website. "I might be able to meet you. I have a thing first."

"Oh? What thing is this?"

I suck in a breath and prepare for the big reveal. "Our new neighbors are coming over for a barbeque."

Callie squeals and I pull the phone away to avoid shattering my eardrum. "No way! Braeden Dalisay is eating dinner at Chez Strong? Am I invited, too?"

In all honesty, I doubt my mom would appreciate Callie's epic flirting with our unsuspecting neighbor. "Better not this time. I'll try to talk you up, though," I say, wondering how I can slide her into the conversation.

"Call me the second he leaves, okay?"

"Okay."

"Pay attention to him, Leanne. No saying you forgot later. Remember. Every. Single. Word."

I release a small sigh. Even my best friend is on Team Braeden.

~

In the kitchen, Mom hums along with her show tunes playlist as she plans the menu, throwing herself into this barbeque to end all barbeques. Dad hauls out his shiny gas grill and hooks up the propane, grumbling to himself the whole time. His lack of technology skills also extends to the operation of home appliances and outdoor cooking tools.

I work alongside Mom, chopping vegetables and following her recipe for poppy seed dressing while she washes Bibb lettuce and arranges it in individual salad bowls before turning them over to me for the finishing touches.

"Only three grape tomatoes per serving." Mom checks over my work, like we're preparing a dinner at the White

House. "They're mainly a garnish."

When the smell of red onion sticks to my hair and skin, I excuse myself to shower. After straightening and then curling my hair, I change into a denim mini-skirt and sleeveless top. The sight of my puny biceps in the mirror conjures up a comparative image of Braeden's muscular arms. Resolving to add weighted curls to my summer workout routine, I swipe on a second coat of mascara just as the doorbell rings. Dad meets me in the hallway and we stroll downstairs together. Taking in my appearance, he raises an eyebrow.

"I decided to look nice for a change," I say, flipping my hair over my shoulder.

Braeden must also notice something different about me, because his brow furrows into a canyon when I make my grand entrance. Aha! Who's unfriendly now? I probably spent a lot more time getting ready for this welcome to the neighborhood barbeque-party than he did. Grinning widely at the Dalisays, I politely ask about their new house. I'm not favored with a smile from Braeden, but no scowling either. Baby steps, I guess.

Sami tugs on my arm. "Leanne, will you tell me about your miracle now?"

"Uh, sure," I say, throwing my mom a look of panic.

"Why don't you show her the pictures?" Mom squeezes my shoulder. She's well aware of my limited ability to describe the miracle healing experience. With everyone's eyes on me, I lead Sami toward the living room. Braeden follows.

In the far corner of the room, we set up a table where two LED candles flicker. Between them rests a statue of Saint Piera. This time of year, a vase of roses from Mom's garden stands next to the statue and framed photos of me as a child form a semi-circle in the background.

"So, Mom was praying here that night," I begin. "But we didn't have the pictures or the statue. That was back before Mother Piera became a saint."

"Did you feel anything?" Sami asks, not even glancing at the table, completely focused on me.

I bite my lip. I can't lie about this, but I want Sami to feel...satisfied with my story. "Um, I was a baby, so I can't say for sure."

She leans forward, checking out the pictures. "Did you cry when it happened?"

"Not until the next morning. Mom said I woke up screaming. She found me in my crib. I'd pulled myself up to a standing position and was trying to walk."

"You never walked before that night?" Sami speaks in a hushed voice.

"No. The doctors told my parents I'd have trouble learning because of my issues." I pick up a framed series of x-rays. I've distanced myself to the point that I no longer feel more than a slight connection to the images of my spine floating in the black space. But even an untrained eye can tell something's not right, thanks to the big red arrows drawn by the doctor who read the radiology report.

Sami takes the photo from my hand. "Whoa," she says. "What exactly was the problem?"

Braeden moves closer to us and out of the corner of my eye, I catch a muscle jump in his jaw. "Sami, maybe you should—"

I raise my hand, letting him know it's okay. By now, questions like this never upset me. It's more the lack of answers that causes most of my problems. "My spine was...twisted a bit and not properly developed. The doctors were talking about different surgeries to correct it, but...as it turns out, I didn't need an operation."

Sami gives me a sad look. "Oh, Leanne. That must have been painful."

"Yeah, but she's fine now," Braeden says, speaking for the first time. "At least you seem okay. Are you?"

If I wasn't a hundred percent okay, would I dare admit it out loud? Cast doubt on my miracle cure? Though the muscles in my neck tighten, I force myself to nod. "Perfect."

He turns back to the x-ray, studying it intently. "I read somewhere that the church might change the miracle requirement for sainthood."

I can't help but wonder where he would read that sort of information. We never discuss miracle technicalities in theology class—my dad keeps me informed of potential changes to church doctrine affecting my case. "From what I remember, there's leeway in the process, but not much. Sometimes the Pope waives the waiting period for sainthood. And martyrs who die for their faith might only need one verified miracle."

He squints at the photo, like he's trying to solve my miracle mystery. "Medical researchers will probably find out what happened to you one day. I read something in bio class about spontaneous healing. It's an observed phenomenon where the body manages to correct itself."

Sami taps the back of her hand on her brother's chest. "But Leanne's miracle has already been verified." She shoots me an apologetic look. "He loves to debate, even when he knows he's totally wrong."

The difference in their attitudes stuns me into a few beats of silence. "If you want specific details about the Church's procedures, you should ask my dad," I finally say. "He spent a lot of time answering questions from the Vatican's medical experts during the validation process." I lift my chin to meet

Braeden's stare. "If you're really interested."

"This is pretty." Sami steps between us, ending our standoff as she examines the pictures on the table. "I want to set up something like this for Emeline. Will you stop by and look at it when I'm finished?"

When Sami mentions her sister's name, Braeden flinches. A raw emotion crosses his face, then disappears before I take another breath.

I trace my finger over the glass tabletop. "Sure. Just call me when you're ready."

A cloud of gray smoke passes by the window, accompanied by the aroma of charred meat. A sigh escapes from my chest. "Dad must be mauling dinner again. He's the worst cook ever." But Mom never offers a suggestion when he's handling a meal. She learned to hold back her comments and choke down dry steak years ago.

Braeden grips Sami from behind and hefts her in the air. "I'm starving. Let's eat."

She screeches and flails her arms. "Put me down!"

"Keep complaining and I'll drop you," he warns.

"I swear, if you hurt me, then you're dead," she says.

Both of them freeze.

"Wait. That's not what I meant to say. I was kidding, Braeden," Sami whispers.

Braeden unwinds his arms from his sister's waist and sets her down gently. He steps aside and motions for me to walk ahead. I retrace my steps through the kitchen, moving quickly to give them time to recover from whatever just happened. From the sounds of laughter floating in through the window, our parents are enjoying their drinks on the patio. I slide open the glass door and find the four of them passing around a pitcher of sangria, laughing and smiling like old friends.

"How do you like your steaks, kids?" Dad asks, holding up a large pair of tongs.

"Well done," Braeden says, throwing me a sideways glance. I turn my head to hide a smile.

We suffer through Dad's steaks, all of us sitting around a long picnic table. Mr. Dalisay and my dad talk business. Mr. Dalisay does some sort of banking stuff that sounds similar to my Dad's legal stuff. The two of them commiserate about college costs, although with a baseball scholarship, I suppose Braeden will go to school for free.

"Is there a miracle scholarship?" Mr. Dalisay asks Dad and everyone laughs.

"Leanne does well in school," Dad says. "She must be in the running for an academic award of some sort." He turns to me, eyebrows wiggling.

While the dads talk finances, the moms talk gardening. Mom loves to discuss organic foods, prompting Mrs. Dalisay to describe in great detail how she hopes to start a garden this summer and grow tomatoes and zucchini. Sitting across the table from me, Sami fires off questions about Holy Family High while Braeden wolfs down two hunks of steak, a salad, three ears of corn and a bucket-sized serving of baked beans.

By the time Mom unveils dessert—lemon pie—bands of bright pinks and pale blues light up the twilight sky. Dad hands Braeden, Sami, and me skewers and lights the grill again. We toast marshmallows to a crisp and Sami manages to set one on fire. Braeden grabs the skewer from her and blows it out.

Fireflies jet tiny dots of light around the backyard by the time the Dalisays say their farewells.

After much thanking and complimenting Mom's cooking, they disappear across the street into their dark house.

Two minutes later, the upstairs lights switch on.

"What a nice family," Mom says. "Such a shame about losing their daughter."

Dad wraps an arm around Mom's shoulders. "They seem to be holding up okay. On the outside, at least."

But we've all noticed the sadness they carry. It's in the small changes in Braeden's expression. The worried glances Mr. and Mrs. Dalisay exchange. The awkward pauses whenever Sami talks about her sister.

Dad rolls our trash can to the end of the driveway for tomorrow's collection while I wait on the porch for Callie to pick me up. She texted three times to remind me about our movie night.

"How was your dinner with the neighbors?" Callie asks as we drive away, after Dad reminds us to strap on our seatbelts.

"Mostly good, with a few minutes of strange," I say.

I can't shake the way Braeden's skepticism about my miracle cure made me feel...diminished. Like he questioned the validity of my existence. Because everyone associates me with a miracle, this reality has filtered its way into every part of my identity. I don't want to be famous because of it, but if it was taken away, would my life be completely different?

Without my miracle, who am I?

"I need more than *strange*," Callie says. "Remember every word!"

I repeat the three whole sentences Braeden and I exchanged during dinner, deciding not to rehash our miracle debate. But, as I continue to go back over the night, my chest feels hollow. Somehow, Braeden managed to tear through the shield I've carefully built up over the years and found a way to uncover my self-loathing and doubt. He wants an easy explanation. Cold, hard, scientific proof that so many others have searched for and never found.

I've dealt with skeptics before and it's always exhausting. Usually, the disbelievers make a joke or throw out a random, incorrect fact. But I've never had someone look me in the eye and tell me that everything about my life will eventually be revealed as completely false. Even if Braeden was only debating for the sake of arguing a point, the idea that my miracle might be declared invalid one day shakes something inside my heart, if only because a small part of me clings to a seed of doubt and believes he might be right.

Chapter 8

After the late night movie, followed by an hour of catching up with Callie, I'm a continuous stream of yawns on the way to work. My sleep requirements must triple in the summer—it's like my entire body slows down when the temperature soars. At the first intersection, I pause to wait for the walk signal, when a black car pulls up beside me.

"Morning, Leanne. Hop in," Braeden says through the open window.

I wave him off. "Thanks, but I like to walk."

He looks so completely shocked that I stifle a burst of laughter by covering my mouth with my hand.

Leaning out the window to check out my choice of footwear, he asks, "You like hiking over burning asphalt in flip flops?"

The light flips to green and I hurry through the intersection. Braeden coasts for another block, eyes shifting between me and the road.

"Leanne?" he asks when we both stop at the next cross street.

"Yes, Braeden?"

"Would you do me the honor of accompanying me to work this morning?"

I snort. "Why do you need accompaniment?"

"For...company?" He lifts a hand off the wheel to massage his temple, like this conversation is truly causing him pain. "And I won't feel guilty about wasting gas if we carpool."

Darn it. He played the environmental card. I step down from the sidewalk and duck into his car.

"Thank you," I say, but the words carry more of a bite than I'd intended. "But you'd waste less gas if we both walked."

"True, but not happening. It's too hot." He points to my seatbelt. "Click it. Unless you're both miracle girl and invincible girl."

I yank the belt across my waist and jam it in the lock.

Braeden takes off with a heavy press on the gas pedal. "Did I do something wrong?"

I almost bring up our miracle discussion again before deciding I might be oversensitive. "No."

He sniffs. "Do I smell bad?"

I lean closer and inhale the light scent of shaving cream and soap. "I don't think so. But I'm not the best smeller."

"Something else then? You have a strange affliction that requires isolation from new neighbors?"

My mouth falls open, but when our eyes meet, he smiles. Oooh. He's joking.

"I just prefer walking whenever possible. No offense, okay?"

"None taken. But, since I was about to pass you on *my* way to *your* dad's office, I thought I might as well stop."

"Appreciate it. I'd love to reciprocate, but only if you

don't mind riding on the handlebars of my bike."

"I think I'll pass."

Do I hear a hint of amusement in his voice? I wonder what it would take to pull a laugh out of him. Since he's in such a talkative mood, I seize the opportunity to work Callie into the conversation. At the barbeque yesterday, he showed zero interest in that type of discussion.

"Where did you go to school in Eddytown?"

He shoots me a fast, curious glance, like he's surprised I don't already have this information. "I went to St. Edward's Prep, but I'm transferring to Holy Family High with Sami."

"Cool. I'll see you around. At dances and stuff." Wait. Did I just admit I want to hang out with him? At dances? My cheeks start to feel warm.

He shifts in his seat. "I'm not a big fan of school dances. But I'm sure we'll see each other."

"Right. Of course we will. Holy Family is a small school." I strain for something else to say. "Also, I wanted to thank you for helping me get away from that reporter on June eighth."

He presses his lips into a harder line. "Why didn't you want to talk to her?"

I look out the window. "Because I don't have the answers she wants to hear."

"So you run away? Every time?"

"Yeah." I swallow hard. "Does that make me a coward?"

"No. But maybe you should take a second to calm down and regroup."

"Regroup what? I never know what to say to the press. Their questions are ridiculous. 'Tell us what you remember.' I wasn't even one year old. I remember absolutely nothing."

"Have you ever explained that to them?" Braeden asks,

calmly and rationally. I'm beginning to understand why Dad hired him.

"Multiple times. Thousands of times."

We lapse into silence and I can almost hear Braeden's brain working. "How about thank you?"

"Thank the reporters?"

"I was thinking more of a general expression of thanks for your, uh, situation. If I'd been the recipient of a miracle, I'd thank anyone and everyone. Every single day of my life. I'd hand out roses at bus stops. Kiss babies and stuff like that."

"Really? You like to kiss babies?" Maybe that's why I'm not cut out for this miracle business. Babies make me nervous. They cry and barf at the worst possible times.

He coughs into his fist. "Okay, you got me. Baby-kissing isn't my thing. But I'm just saying—"

"I get it." I cut him off. Because, honestly, no one gets it and no matter what he says, he won't come close to describing what I've lived with the past fifteen years. Not that I really expect him, or anyone else to understand. Even my parents have trouble relating to the weight of the attention focused on me.

Before I find a way to switch the conversation to Callie, we're pulling into the office parking lot.

"So, *thank you* for the ride," I say, since gratitude is apparently high on his list of important personality traits.

"Thank *you* for not making me look like a jerk, driving beside you for the last two miles," Braeden answers, twirling a key ring around his finger as we step out of the car. A glint of sunlight brightens his dark eyes as he pulls the door open and holds it for me. The air conditioning greets us and my chest expands to accommodate a full breath.

Behind the front desk, Celeste beams like a tall, bright sun in her yellow dress and newly braided hair.

"Leanne Strong. We have a major predicament in this office and I've been told to take it up with you. Where are my files?" She holds up her empty in-box. "Everything is gone. Disappeared."

Braeden runs his hand over his face, probably hiding his smile.

"Hey, Celeste. Did you have a nice vacation?" I tug my hair into a knot on top of my head and secure it with a band, preparing for work. Explaining my paperless filing system to her is going to make for a long, possibly intensely frustrating day. Her mouth opens to respond just as she notices Braeden standing next to me. The slight pause tells me she's impressed by our new employee.

"And this must be Braeden. Mr. Strong told me all about you." Celeste circles around the desk and picks up a stack of law journals. "He'd like you to read and summarize the flagged articles."

"Nice," Braeden says, excited by his assignment.

Celeste turns to me. "Leanne, you can alphabetize and file the latest docket reports. After you tell me what happened to my papers."

"Seriously? He gets to read and I get to alphabetize?"

Celeste blinks at my tirade. "Your father said Braeden is interested in the law." Long pause, as she searches for a polite way to describe my less than stellar work attitude. "And you're a very good alphabetizer," she finishes.

Which is true. I'm the fastest filer in the office. Two years of library shelving have improved my accuracy.

"She's also highly skilled at document shredding," Braeden offers in a deadpan voice.

I burst out laughing when Celeste brings her hand to her

heart and flutters her eyelashes.

"Don't worry, I didn't shred anything important. I scanned your inbox into the electronic folders on your desktop," I tell her. "I'll show you how I did it. After that, can I type some client letters?"

Celeste shrugs. "If your dad says it's okay. I have quite the backlog today. And Mia's busy researching the Pemberton slip-and-fall case."

While Celeste and Braeden become further acquainted, I dart into Dad's office, upset over my sense of unimportance. Dad says he loves having me help him, right? So why am I so easily replaced and relegated to grunt work?

When I knock on his door, he hangs up the phone and smiles. "Hi, Love Bug."

My look of horror erases his easy grin.

"No nicknames at work," I say through gritted teeth. "Why is Braeden reading and summarizing law articles?"

Dad appears confused. "Sorry, did you want to read them? Last year, when I asked if you wanted to prepare case summaries, you mentioned something about preferring to file papers rather than read and summarize the boring words on them."

"Well, yeah, but you can get anyone to file. So, if I'm not really helping you...I just don't want to be a burden." I plop into a chair across from him.

Dad reaches for a pen and taps it on his desk. "Actually, you are helping me a great deal, Leanne. If you didn't spend every summer in the office, I'd probably need to hire someone else. Celeste spends a lot of time on the phone." His nice way of saying she isn't the most efficient filer. "She's a good...talker. She puts clients at ease."

"Right now she's not very agreeable. Braeden may have led

her to believe that I shredded her entire in-box."

Dad smirks. "The fallout begins."

"I'll handle it," I say quickly. "But, Dad, really—I can help with law stuff too. Whatever you need."

He leans across his desk. "Don't tell anyone, but I'm trying to help Braeden. If he's interested in the law he needs to learn about the less exciting aspects of the job." Dad picks up a small folder sitting the desk in front of him. "I already have summaries of the cases he's reading, but I'm interested in seeing what he comes up with."

I smile. "Okay. Thanks. Just wanted to make sure."

I retreat from the office, ready for a day-long marathon of document scanning instruction with Celeste.

~

As quitting time approaches, my stomach churns. After the unexpected ride to work, should I expect Braeden to drive me home? Are we something like friends now?

"Do you have a ride back to Chestnut Street?" Braeden breezes into the file room at five o'clock. "I'm meeting a friend in my old neighborhood."

"I can walk, it's not a problem. Thanks again for picking me up this morning."

Seeming preoccupied, he glances at the buzzing clock and rushes out with barely a good-bye.

After he leaves, I add paper to the copier, but misfeed the stack and spend extra time unjamming a paper crumpled into an accordion. Why does Braeden throw me off so much? Twice today, I missed the chance to bring up Callie when he cut away before I was able to come up with something that sounded casual, yet deliberate enough to pull information from him. I sling my purse over my shoulder and switch off the lights, still wondering about our latest copy room run-in. Is the friend he's meeting tonight a girlfriend? Guys don't hang out in packs of two, do they? I need to consult Callie about this—she's the best at interpreting boy-speak.

Chapter 9

When I leave the house for work, Braeden's car blocks the end of my driveway. Through the window, I spy his long limbs sprawled across the driver's seat, which is tipped all the way back. His eyes are shut and his chest moves up and down when he takes a slow breath. I pull the door open and slide inside, watching him jolt awake.

"Hey. Long night?" My morning voice sounds like it needs a tune-up.

He yawns and blinks the sleep out of his eyes. "I watched the late game. It went into extra innings."

"And you stayed awake for the last pitch rather than check the scores this morning?"

"I was wired. It was exciting," he says, using a word I rarely attach to the game of baseball.

He checks the rear view mirror before firing up the engine.

"You could have slept in a couple more minutes. If I'm not walking to work, we can leave later. Dad starts paying us at nine."

Braeden tilts his head side to side, stretching his neck. "We can stop for coffee, but I like to leave extra time."

I cast a curious glance his way, then motion toward the empty road ahead. "Are you worried about a traffic incident?"

"I like to be prepared," he says. "To me, work is like baseball. I need to be ready to step on the field at game time. Give myself time to stretch and throw."

Hands raised, I curl and flex my fingers. "This is how I warm up for filing. And my dad warms up with a sesame bagel and the daily crossword."

"There you go. Same concept."

"Sure. I guess." I hold back my opinion on the actual importance of the work my father assigns to us. I wouldn't want Braeden to be discouraged. "Your sister claims you're an undercover nerd."

His eyebrows fly up. "Sami called me a nerd? She's the one who reads five-hundred page classics for fun."

I picture the brother and sister sitting on the couch late at night, one reading and one watching baseball. There's no doubt in my book-loving mind who's having more fun, but now isn't the time for that debate with Braeden. "How's your sister adjusting? With the move and everything."

He flicks on the turn signal and checks for oncoming traffic before blowing out some fast words. "She's uh, busy with her mini-shrine set-up. She wants to top yours, I think."

"Oh," I say, and then, "That's good, I guess."

Braeden throws me a sidelong glance. "I'll tell her you've been busy, too. She asks about you all the time."

"Really?" I wonder if she's waiting for me to make the next move and knock on her door. It's not a huge thing for me to walk across the street and visit. We've texted a few times since the family barbeque, but I could make more of an effort. "I'd like to drop by after work. Maybe we can trade books. And I owe her a haircut."

Braeden peels his wide eyes from the road. "She wants you to cut her hair?"

The tone of his voice prompts me to peek in the rear view mirror, expecting a tangled atrocity. Despite the extra humidity-induced waves, I'm actually having a good hair day. "I know what I'm doing."

"Sure you do," he says in a voice that seems to say the opposite. "Maybe messing around with her hair will take her mind off..." He doesn't finish the sentence. "Do you need a ride home?"

"If it's going to be a hundred degrees again, yes. If you don't have plans."

If he notices the heavy suggestion behind my words, he doesn't react. "Nope."

"No friend to visit?" I'm pushing hard, but telling myself it's for Callie's benefit.

"You can walk home if you want," he says, his voice perfectly calm.

"Either way is fine."

Our stalemate lasts for three blocks.

"Why do you care about my plans?" he asks. From his tone, I sense he's more amused than angry.

Sigh. Callie is going to owe me for this. "I was just making conversation."

"So am I and I don't recall asking about your social life."

I lift my chin. "You told Sami I might be out on a date last Friday."

"I was trying to help you out. I didn't think you wanted to spend all night with her and Gabby."

But why did he say a date? He could have said out with

friends, or any other excuse.

"I don't mind hanging out with your sister. You didn't need to make up an excuse for me."

"Okay, then. From now on, expect a lot more visits from Sami." He smiles and I notice that one of his front teeth is slightly crooked. "And since you're so interested, last night I had an... appointment. Afterward, my buddy Zach and I went to the batting cages."

Appointment is still a vague term, but I'll let it slide. Why is small talk so hard? Or is it only hard with Braeden? "Do you play baseball outside of school?"

Keeping his eyes on the road, he nods. "Summer leagues, select tournaments. I might start practicing with the Holy Family guys, too. Coach called me when he found out I'd moved cross-county."

After successfully pulling so much information from him, I feel compelled to keep the baseball conversation going. "I hear Coach Trent's a bear when it comes to practice," I say, recalling complaints from guys in my homeroom.

"He's okay. I like to practice, anyway."

"You like to practice and warm up? Do you also like to study calculus and write term papers?"

He raises a hand to stop me. "I see where you're going with this. Yes, yes and yes. I won the geography bee in middle school and was a runner up for the spelling bee, too. I can also tell you the middle name of every American president and recite Pi to the twentieth decimal."

I snap my fingers. "Lincoln."

"Old Abe? He didn't have a middle name."

"Ha. You don't know what you're talking about."

"Look it up."

I pull out my phone and run a quick search. "Shoot.

You're right. Okay, Monroe."

"None again."

"This is very educational. I had no idea that middle names were optional for dead presidents."

"A lot of the early ones only had a first and last name. You hit two of them. Want to try again?"

"Gerald Ford?" I pull a name out of thin air. I don't know if I remember many more of these guys.

"He's Rudolph."

I crack a smile. "Congratulations, Braeden Dalisay, you are a complete and total history nerd."

"And yet, here you are, riding to work with me."

"Because it would've been rude to walk around your car when you completely blocked my driveway."

With this sort of back and forth chatter, I temporarily forget how awkward I feel around Braeden. I'm never sure if he's still upset about the first day we met, when I acted so ungrateful about my miracle. Pushing all thoughts of that unfortunate incident aside, I spend the rest of the ride trying to stump him, but he's definitely spent a lot of time researching presidential middle names.

"Tomorrow, be prepared for a geography quiz," I tell him when he turns into the parking lot behind Dad's office.

Braeden cuts the engine and our eyes meet and hold. "Don't worry, miracle girl. I'll be ready for whatever you want to throw at me."

~

Later in the morning, Braeden strides into the file room to use the copy machine.

We maneuver around each other in the tight space, carefully avoiding physical contact. While he waits for the machine to do its job, I gather my courage. “Hey, can I ask you something?”

The overhead lighting shines down on him, spotlighting the discomfort on his face. “Uh... sure.”

I force out a light laugh which only seems to increase the tension between us. “I’m actually asking for someone else. She’s my best friend, and—”

Before I bring up Callie’s name, Mia barges in the file room.

“Hello, hello, everyone.” She holds up Braeden’s case summaries. “Can we talk about how awesome you are? Your write-ups are just as good as any first year law student’s work.”

Braeden smiles. “Thanks, Mia.”

She tilts her head toward the door. “Are you busy now? I have a few minor critiques. Very minor.”

He starts to follow her out, then doubles back to pick up his copies, which he forgot about in all the excitement. “Catch you later, Leanne?”

I wave. “Sure.”

Braeden’s definitely smart, on top of being an awesome athlete. To be honest, I don’t know how Callie can assume he doesn’t have a girlfriend. Or, at the very least, have tons of girls willing to fill the role. I just need some sort of confirmation to convince her to stop obsessing over him.

Around eleven o’clock, Dad emerges from his office. “Great work today, everyone.”

I wonder if his secretly installed spy cameras are malfunctioning. From what I saw, Celeste spent a good hour chatting on the phone with a repeat client. After spending ten minutes discussing case summaries, Braeden and Mia compared cars

(Mia's shopping for one and apparently Braeden's recent purchase makes him an expert). I sent three faxes to judges and picked up the phone twice while Celeste talked on the other line.

Dad smiles at all of us. "I want to buy everyone lunch. Celeste, do you have a menu for The Snack Bar?"

Celeste digs around in her desk, pulling out stacks of random papers that make my insides cringe before finally producing a menu for a café in town where every sandwich has a trendy name.

I order my favorite, the San Diego Chicken, a flat bread stuffed with avocado. Braeden asks for the Flamethrower, which comes with extra-hot buffalo sauce.

"You're a brave man," Dad tells him, slapping him on the back. "I haven't had a Flamethrower in years."

An hour later, we gather in the conference room, waiting for Braeden to unwrap his lunch. Celeste chews on her fingernail and Dad drums his fingers on the tabletop. The paper around the Flamethrower crinkles as Braeden removes the sandwich and the air ignites with the scent of cayenne pepper and hot sauce.

We all lean in when he takes the first bite.

Immediately, he launches into a coughing fit. I can practically see smoke blow out of his ears.

Mia cracks up. "Red alert, Leanne!"

I toss him a water bottle and he snags it. I give him a pitying look as he gulps his way through the entire bottle.

While Braeden recovers, Mia entertains us by chattering on about casework and writs.

"I love the ins and outs of the law," she proclaims, digging into her salad. "The way justice is administered by juries and judges. What do you think you'll specialize in, Braeden?"

"When I graduated, I couldn't wait to work for a big city firm," Dad cuts in. "A year later, I was dreaming about hanging up a shingle and working for myself."

"I'd like to deal with environmental issues," Braeden says. He exhales a long breath as he continues to air out his mouth. "Or maybe work for the district attorney's office."

"Often, you don't get much of a choice right out of the gate. But let me tell you, if you work for a big law firm, don't plan on having a social life. The hours are brutal." Dad shivers at the memory of his first job.

"Leanne, do you have career plans? Or are you too young to think about the future?" Mia asks, like she doesn't know Braeden's only a year older than me.

I pick a sliver of onion out of my sandwich. "I'm not sure yet."

"Leanne might do better working backward," Dad says, nudging his way into the discussion, as usual. "She likes to read and language arts is her best subject. But after working here for the last few summers, she's pretty much ruled out a legal career. And she doesn't like being a public figure. She avoids all kinds of reporters, so I'd say journalism is a no-go."

"Dad. Stop." I shoot him a red-hot glare. This is why Mom warned me against working in the family business. He's way too comfortable around me and it's embarrassing.

"But you're great with technology," he presses on, directing a broad grin my way. Payback time has arrived. He crumples his sandwich wrapper into a ball and chucks it into the trash can. "Maybe you'll travel around the country and force unsuspecting dinosaurs to adopt a paperless environment."

"I'm trying to help you," I insist, gripping my empty water bottle to keep my frustration in check. "You're ruthlessly killing a lot of innocent trees."

"Sami likes hanging out with you. Maybe you'd like to work with kids? Or something in the medical field?" Braeden suggests.

"Nursing. You have the temperament," Celeste says. "But you hate blood, don't you, Leanne? You nearly faint when you get a paper cut."

Mia straightens in her chair, eyes bright, unable to hold back from adding her thoughts. "You don't even need a real career to make money. You like helping people, and you'd think that with your miracle history, you could travel the world and—"

"And do what? You think people would pay to see me stand around, doing nothing? You think that's how it works?" I ask, floored by her statement. "People have expectations of things I can't give them. If they took the time to understand and get to know who I really am, they'd be disappointed. So, yeah, I need to work, just like everyone else on this planet."

Dad rises out of his chair, about to intervene, but Mia seems to realize she misspoke.

"Sorry, Leanne, I shouldn't have said that. I know you wouldn't take advantage of your miracle. But I don't think you can pretend it didn't happen, either."

I wait for Dad to stand up for me, but he only looks on with a sad smile. He feels some amount of guilt about my unintended fame, which isn't something he should feel.

"I've never denied it," I say. "But I won't use it to gain something I'm not entitled to, either."

Chapter 10

I spend the rest of the afternoon hiding in the file room, unsure of what to say to Braeden. Yes, I've held back on certain aspects of my life because of my miracle. Opening up to people, becoming close friends with anyone other than Callie. Dating. Talking to Sami and anyone else who seems to think I'm special. Because I'm not. I didn't do anything to call up a miracle. I'm lucky, maybe. But not special.

The copy machine begins to whir, sparking to life after spending most of the day in sleep mode. Paper spits out too fast and then stops. I hear a crunching noise coming from the feeder and yank the power cord from the wall, letting out an exasperated sigh. Paper jams are the worst. I lift the top and spend ten minutes picking out pieces of crinkled paper.

While the machine warms up again, I shelve a stack of files Celeste left on the work table before lunch, lining up the folders according to case number. One file is missing a label, so I flip it open to check the documents inside. Instead of the usual case summary, I spy a brochure about the Saint Piera Shrine. Followed by architectural plans. Zoning ordinances.

Construction permits.

What is this?

Apparently, my very own father was the legal counselor representing Spring River in the zoning hearings. I flip through pages of building rules and regulations. Behind those seemingly endless words are scanned images of similar shrines around the world. I spread out the pictures of marble statues commissioned by the Vatican and try to guess who they represent. Definitely a Blessed Mother and a Saint Piera. Maybe a Mother Katherine Drexel and a Mother Theresa.

"Ready to go?" At the sound of Braeden's voice, I jump. My knee bumps the table leg and the file slides away, hitting the floor with a dull thud and a flurry of loose papers. Braeden bends to help me pick everything up and his eyebrows lift when he notices a picture of Saint Piera.

"I was just...yes, I'm ready." I don't even know what to say. Braeden clears his throat and hands the picture to me. I cram everything back in the folder and stuff the file into a pocket of empty shelf space, abandoning my organization plans until tomorrow.

We leave the office together and push into the steamy late afternoon sun. After our easy conversation this morning, the aftermath of Mia's comments and the discovery of the Saint Piera file seem to add cooler layers to our unsteady friendship.

I want him to know that I'm not a horrible, ungrateful person. That I wouldn't ignore the chance to help others if it came along, but so far, I haven't found the best way to do that. I don't want to take advantage of a gift I was given. I'm a good person who tries to do the right thing, though sometimes it may not appear that way.

When we're out of the building, away from my father, I take a deep breath. "Mia doesn't know me as well as she thinks. I don't try to hide anything." Although the first day we met, Braeden caught me running away from a reporter. "I mean, when I can answer questions, I will. But I don't always have the answers."

Braeden's expression tightens. "Sometimes, when you don't talk about something, it turns it into an even bigger deal. Maybe just admit what you don't know and move on."

I laugh nervously. "Good point. But I don't want you to think I'm purposely hiding something. I don't have a secret superpower. I'm just a normal person."

He steps ahead of me and opens the car door, indicating that I should take a seat. He circles the car and slides in his side. "What did you want to ask me earlier, in the file room, before Mia interrupted us?"

I stammer for a full ten seconds before I manage to say, "I was asking for a friend. She wanted to know if you have a girlfriend."

His starts the car and checks the rear view mirror. "No girlfriend. What about you? Are you seeing anyone?"

"No, but I have reasons for not getting involved with guys around here."

I clasp my shaking hands together. Neither of us speaks again until we're close to Chestnut Street.

"Can I guess why you don't have a boyfriend?" he asks. Though I can't bear to look at him right now, I hear the smile in his voice.

"Sure, give it a go."

"You're in love with someone who's unattainable. Like a movie star or rock star."

A snicker escapes me. As if. "Wrong."

"Your parents promised you a new car if you wait until college to start dating?"

"Wrong again. They're not like that."

He shoots me a curious look. "It has something to do with the miracle then."

I cut my eyes to the window. "My whole life has something to do with the miracle." I gather my strength and turn back to him. "Is now a good time for me to stop in and see Sami?"

Braeden taps his fingers on the steering wheel. "Yeah, she's home. She texted me earlier and I told her you might stop by."

He pulls into the driveway and jumps out of the car ahead of me. When I follow him inside, he calls his sister.

Sami pokes her head out of the kitchen. "Hey, Leanne. Wait 'til I tell Gabby you were here. She said you didn't really like me, you were just being nice 'cause of Brae—"

"Of course I like you," I cut her off. Is Braeden so irresistible that Sami assumes every girl who hangs out with her is secretly crushing on him?

At the sight of his sister, Braeden backs away. "I'll leave you two alone. I'm sure you have a lot of girl stuff to talk about." He streaks up the stairs, two at a time, like he's afraid we'll try to pierce his ears or braid his hair.

"I'm glad he's gone," Sami says, watching him practically flee into his bedroom. "I'm tired of hearing about his curve and slider. He's so obsessed with baseball."

"He also likes to talk about presidential middle names."

Sami's mouth twists into a smile. "He loves to show off. Poor Leanne."

"At least one of you likes to talk about books. What are you reading now?"

She points to the coffee table in the front room, littered with teen fan magazines. "Just fun stuff. I've been in a reading slump lately." She picks up a framed photo of two girls in sequined costumes. "Em and I used to dance, ballet and jazz, before..." Her chin quivers. "Anyway, I don't dance anymore." She sets the frame back on the table. "I should unpack some of this stuff. My mom says the rest of the house has to look nice, but we keep all the boxes we haven't opened in here."

I glance around at the stacks of boxes, neatly labeled according to contents, like books or pictures. "I can help. I like to organize."

"If you have time." She casts a doubtful look my way.

"Tell me where to start."

We spend an hour unpacking boxes and organizing her book collection. Sami finds her yearbooks and shows me some of her friends from Eddytown, including the boy who kissed her good-bye the night before she moved. "That's over now," she says with a sigh. "Have you ever kissed anyone, Leanne?"

I admit that I have.

She sets the yearbook on an empty shelf. "How many times?"

"Once or twice," I say. "Maybe more. Not real kisses though. More...experimenting. I don't really date."

She swings her attention back to me, her forehead puckering. "Why not? You're so pretty. I wish boys looked at me the way they look at you."

My face warms. Sami's only seen me with one boy: her brother. But from my perspective, Braeden rarely acknowledges my existence when his sister is close by.

"Boys don't think of me as someone to go out with. Most of the guys around here know who I am and they treat me differently because of it."

"What do you mean? Who are you?" Sami stares at me expectantly. "Oh, are you talking about the miracle?" Her mouth presses into a thin line. "I can understand that, I guess. I was intimidated by you at first."

"You shouldn't be. I don't think I'm an intimidating person."

"No, you're just...quiet. But I can see why people would think something different about you."

I sigh. "People mean well, but they say the worst things some times. Including me."

"What have you said?" Sami looks surprised.

"When I first met your mother and brother...before I knew about your sister...I was rude," I confess.

Sami lifts a narrow shoulder. "You didn't know about Em. No one blames you." She sinks into the sofa, studying the half-filled bookshelves. "Em and I looked alike. Teachers, neighbors, even our friends would mix up our names. Now, no one talks about her. I wonder if they forget...or they just don't want to upset me."

I take a seat near her, but still leave some space between us. "How are you doing? Was moving away hard?"

"In some ways, yes. I felt like we left Emeline behind all over again." She looks at her hands. "You shouldn't worry about dating, or whatever. Braeden doesn't go out much, either. Baseball takes up most of his life outside of school."

"He said he doesn't have a girlfriend."

"Not right now," Sami agrees. "Girls call him. At dinner, his phone buzzes and Mom tells him to shut it down. But there's no one important. I would know if there was."

"Braeden tells you about his girlfriends?"

She breaks into a smile. "I ask a lot of questions. Sometimes I wear him down."

Did I ever mention how much I love Sami?

I tilt my head toward a stack of boxes stacked in a corner. "Are those more books?"

She follows my line of sight and her eyes dim. "That's Em's stuff. We haven't decided where to put it yet." She glances at me with a hopeful expression. "I should at least look through it. We can add her books to the shelves behind the table with her picture. Mom said she'd buy some candles like yours, to decorate."

I turn away from her, trying to hide the dampness in my eyes. How dare I cry over someone I never knew? Because I see what she left behind. As Sami and I unpack the first box, her sister becomes more familiar to me. From the pictures Sami pulls out, the girls do look alike, but Emeline has Braeden's darker hair.

"She was in fifth grade," Sami says, running her fingertips over her sister's smiling image. "The baby of the family. But not spoiled, you know? Just happy." Somewhere in the house a door closes and Sami seems to snap out of her sadness. "My mom's having a bad day. She's tired."

"I should go. I didn't mean to intrude—"

"You didn't. I was happy to see you." Sami places the picture back in the box. "The house wasn't completely quiet, for a change."

"Okay. Good." I swallow hard. "If you like to read, I have tons of books. Most of them are from school, but...maybe we can start our own secret book club."

A faint smile flickers on her face. "Thanks, Leanne. Text me the titles and I'll let you know what I haven't read yet."

"I'll pack up whatever you want and haul it over here." I motion toward the empty bookshelves. "You still have space. And I promise to bring the scissors I save for hair cutting next time."

Sami flips her long hair. "Definitely. I need to do something with this mess."

When she walks me to the front door, I finally pick up on the extreme quiet Sami talked about. I realize that since I walked in the door, I haven't heard a cell phone ring. There's no music playing, or sound from the television.

"If you want to hang out, knock for me," I tell her. "Or send a text. Anytime. I mean it."

Outside, Braeden is packing the trunk of his car with baseball gear. He's changed out of the button-down shirt and gray pants he wore to work and into a white baseball uniform. Wearing a blue baseball cap, with his shirt untucked, he looks less serious. Almost like a different person. I pause to watch him, wanting to memorize his face: the smooth slope of his cheekbones, the long, dark eyelashes and the shape of his nose in profile.

He shuts the car door and turns, catching me standing on the porch for no good reason.

"Pick you up tomorrow?" he asks.

After an uncomfortable time delay, I squeak out an answer. "Sure. See you then."

I dart away, not daring to look back, half-wondering if he's watching me go.

~

Braeden barely says hey when I slide in the front seat, and since I'm struggling to keep my eyelids propped open, his low-key greeting doesn't bother me in the least. I lean my head against the window and nearly fall back to sleep when he brakes at a light and turns to me. "If you're not in a hurry to get to work, we could drive by the shrine."

Adrenaline flies through me, faster than a mega-dose of caffeine. My fingers wrap around the medal dangling from my neck. "No. I mean, thanks, but no."

A muscle jumps in his jaw. "Weren't you looking at the pictures in the office yesterday?"

"Because I found the file by mistake." And I still haven't confronted Dad about it.

Braeden's dark eyes narrow. "Really? You didn't know your father was working on the case?"

"No." A pause. "Did you?"

Silence. It's enough of an answer.

I check the time on my phone. One extra turn and this can be over, for now.

"Just go. We're almost there," I say.

But I'm not ready for this. Panic rises like a slow-moving tidal wave in my chest. I've avoided the construction site at all costs and seeing the shrine makes everything seem real. Too real. The story of my miracle isn't a fairy tale told by my parents anymore—it's being brought to life in front me.

"Leanne?" Braeden's voice sounds far away. "Leanne, are you sick or something?"

"I'm not ready for this." I blurt out what's going through my mind without stopping to think. "I can't be what everyone wants me to be."

The framed-out shrine appears ahead of us. I cut my eyes away from the scene. I've seen enough.

Braeden presses the gas and makes a quick turn. "Who's everyone? What do they want you to be?"

"Monsignor told the reporters I'll be at the dedication. He wants me to talk about my experience. But I've never done that before and I don't know how I'll be able to do it in front of thousands of people."

I wait for Braeden's reaction, disappointment, more doubt about my miracle, or even a calm, level-headed response to my dramatic behavior.

"I'm sorry, Leanne. I didn't meant to upset you," he says in a low voice, turning the car away from the shrine.

He doesn't say anything else as we roll through town. There's just the hum of the engine, a tap of the brakes, and a parting of the ways after he pulls into the parking lot.

~

Callie calls during her lunch break, yelling above the happy screams of mini-campers. "Leanne! We missed you at youth group last night."

"I forgot," I lie. I've purposely skipped all church activities since the shrine announcement. Truth be told, I'm afraid of running into Monsignor without my parents acting as a buffer.

"So there's this party tonight—"

"No."

She huffs through the phone. "Do you even know what I'm asking?"

"We've been friends long enough. Who wants to meet the miracle girl?"

"One guy in particular. Jake Maddaloni. His dad's the architect who designed the shrine. When I mentioned your name, he asked if you were the girl in the big wall mural."

My palms start to sweat. "There's a painting of me?"

"Baby you, but yes. According to Jake, the artwork was commissioned six months ago."

I grab Dad's shrine file from the shelf and flip it open. The original log date is over three years old. "How did I miss this?"

"What did you miss?"

"Nothing. Sorry, what were you saying? Before the part about the mural."

"The party tonight. Please, Leanne. Jake's friend Gavin is super-cute."

"What about Braeden?"

"Did you ask him about me yet?"

"Not about you, specifically. But I have answers to some of your questions." Thanks to Sami. "He isn't dating anyone right now."

"Awesome. Bring him with you."

"I can't do that! I thought you liked Braeden. Now there's a Gavin in the picture?"

"They're both cute. Hmmm, maybe if I talk to Gavin tonight, and finally meet Braeden, I can make a decision about which one is the better potential boyfriend material." I hear a thunk and Callie telling the kids to line up for their next activity. "Sorry, Leanne, gotta go. You should ask Braeden to drive you to the party. You don't have a car, so it's a perfect excuse."

"I'm not asking Braeden for a ride."

"What about me?"

And here he is, leaning against the doorway of the file room. Because of course I'm so wrapped up in my phone conversation that I forgot to keep an eye out for the subject of said conversation, who happens to spend most of the day working less than ten feet away from me.

"Nothing," I say before turning my attention back to Callie. "Talk to you later."

I jam my phone in my purse, but not before a text buzzes in from Callie, pleading with me to meet her at the party.

Meanwhile, Braeden's waiting for an explanation. "If it was nothing, you'd tell me," he says.

Right. He's so right. I need to answer him, to see this through for Callie's sake. She'll never stop asking about him if I don't. "My friend Callie invited me to a party tonight and she mentioned something about bringing you along." I fumble for a casual excuse. "Um, because you're new in town."

He tilts his head and the ceiling light skims over his deep brown eyes, giving them an amber glow. "Cool. What time should I pick you up?"

I raise my hand to stop him. "Not necessary. I told her no."

"Why?" Frowning, Braeden keeps his eyes on me as he steps up to the copier.

"Because I don't want to go."

He taps the start button and scrolls through the touch menu. The machine beeps and his eyes narrow, like he's playing chess and can't figure out his next move.

I flip the top up for him. "Paper goes here. Lined up with the arrows."

"Oh, right. I knew that." He sets a paper on the glass, closes the top and presses the touch screen again. The machine bursts to life, launching into warm-up mode. While we wait, he turns to me. "Why don't you want to go? Do you have other plans?"

The walls of the file room seem to shrink a bit. "No, but—"

"Tonight's my only night this week without a game or practice. And you need a ride." He studies me with a purpose. How long was he eavesdropping? "I'm happy to help you out."

Before I fire off a round of protests, it strikes me that Braeden might want to meet new people, possibly make a few connections with the Holy Family crowd before school starts. Since he's been driving me to work, maybe I should return the favor and introduce him to some of my friends.

I snatch his copies from the feeder and hand them to him. "Is 7:30 okay? It's a swim party."

Braeden's mouth twitches and my heart stirs in my chest, like it's awakening from a hundred-year sleep. The look on his face...he's almost...happy.

"You've got yourself a date," he says and disappears before I disagree with his shocking description.

Chapter 11

"Not a date. Clearly not a date." A delivery for Judge Peters sits in Celeste's outbox, so I burn off my anxious energy with a walk to the courthouse, braving ninety degrees to avoid another run-in with Braeden at the copy machine.

After my heartbeat stabilizes, I return to work.

Braeden passes me in the hallway and I stumble back against the wall, holding my breath until he disappears into the conference room. I can't go out on a date with him. Why did he assume that's what I was asking? I specifically mentioned Callie's name and said she thought I should bring him with me tonight. None of this was my idea.

This is so messed up.

When I slink back to the file room, the fax machine chirps and spits out long pages of legalese. I grab each page as it rolls out of the feeder and fasten everything together with a paper clip. As long as I'm worked up, I may as well channel my fury and talk to Dad about the shrine.

I drop the fax on his desk and stand in front of him, hands on my hips.

"Yes, Leanne?" His eyes move left to right as he reads the first few paragraphs of the document before setting it aside to focus on me.

"I found a file. A *shrine* file." I jab my index finger on the glossy wood surface of his desk. "Apparently you, Attorney Strong, are the town's main point of contact for all legal matters."

He looks up at me with a guilt-filled expression. "Mom and I decided not to tell you about it until the final approval went through. Then Monsignor beat us to it when he announced everything on TV. If you had read through the case history in the file, you'd understand how much of an uphill battle this was. Labor contracts, construction permits, zoning clearances...It took years.."

I move my hands off my hips and make a helpless gesture. "And you were waiting for me to read a case file rather than just tell me before I started working this summer?"

Dad breathes out a laugh. "No, I was trying to find a good time to tell you what was going on, but that never happened, did it?"

"It would have been nice to know something. Like three years ago, when the whole thing started."

"I'm sorry, Leanne." He shifts in his squeaky chair, folding his hands together on top of his desk. "The shrine started out as a small idea, one thing led to another, and it snowballed." Shooting me a wry smile, he adds, "We could always move."

"Oh, no. *We* are not moving. I'm leaving for college in two years. You and Mom can stay here and deal with the year-round visitors."

With a sigh, he tugs at the knot on his tie. "Sounds fair. Are you still considering making an appearance at the dedication?"

"Honestly? No. Braeden and I drove past the shrine today and...it was hard." I glance out the window at the bright blue sky.

Dad grins. "You and Braeden, huh?"

I lift a pen off his desk and roll it between my fingers and thumb. "What does that mean? Me and Braeden?"

"Don't think I haven't noticed who's driving you to work."

Huffing out a breath, I drop the pen and head for the door. "This is why we can't work together."

Dad's laughter follows me out of his office.

~

"Big plans tonight?" Mom catches me in her room, trying on a new bathing suit in front of the full length mirror.

"Just a swim party with some people from the youth group," I say, knowing she'll approve any activity associated with church. "I'll be home early."

The doorbell rings and Mom's brows slant together. "Is Callie picking you up?"

To avoid answering, and also because I'm running late, I dash back to my room and grab my sling bag.

Mom strolls downstairs and opens the front door. "Hello, Braeden. Mr. Strong's not home from work yet. Can I help you?"

I shove my feet into flip flops, shimmy into my cover-up, and race downstairs just as my mother realizes what's going on.

Her head bobs back and forth between me and my not-a-date. "Leanne?"

"Braeden's driving me to the party." I aim a pleading look at her. *Please don't torture me about this.* "Okay?"

She swallows hard and it's totally noticeable. "Yes, wonderful."

But it's not. She thinks this is a date. My first date. Knowing Mom, she wanted to play an important role in picking out my outfit, helping me with makeup, and doing all sorts of mother-daughter pre-date bonding stuff. She thinks I cut her out of a life-altering event, and I'll pay for my scheming when I return home later tonight.

As I slip past her, she slides her arms around me and gives me a hug. "Be good." Seriously, does she have to embarrass me now? Then, to further increase my humiliation, she turns to Braeden. "Did you join the youth group, Braeden?"

"No, Mrs. Strong, I'm busy with baseball this summer, but I offered to drive Leanne because she didn't have a ride and she really wanted to go to the party."

I twist around, taking in his completely serious expression.

Mom looks pleased. "How nice of you. Usually I don't allow Leanne to drive alone in cars with boys, but tonight I'll make an exception."

Did I mention that I never date? Could this be one of many reasons why?

Before she asks any more ridiculous questions, I cut and run. Braeden hurries to keep up.

"Wear a seatbelt and be home by curfew," Mom calls after us.

"Right. Curfew. Bye." I duck into the car.

Still gazing back at my house, Braeden fires up the ignition. "Are you sure this is okay? Your mom seems a little worried."

"She must think you're dangerous," I retort, then instantly regret my choice of words.

But Braeden tips his head back and laughs. And holy wow,

if I thought his smile was heart-shattering, the light on his face now might be bright enough to melt rock into lava.

"If she's praying for my demise, I'm in trouble. She's got proven spiritual power on her side. Where to?"

I pull my phone out of my bag and recite the address Callie texted me. While Braeden's focused on the road, I steal a peek at his new-looking navy blue bathing suit. He's also wearing a sleeveless shirt, exposing his biceps. When he catches me looking and gives me a shy smile, I feel like the Earth has started to rotate backwards, though I'm the only person who seems to notice. This is not the Braeden I know. Smiley, laughing...attractive. I mean, the attractiveness potential was obvious from the get-go, but combined with this new sunny personality, he's transformed into someone I could easily develop a crush on. But I can't go there with him. We work together every day and too many people are watching us. Plus, Callie. I chant her name in my head several times to help shield myself against Braeden's smile.

"I'm sorry for dragging you out tonight," I say, hoping to reinforce our friendly, but definitely not-on-a-date status. "I just need to make an appearance to keep my friends happy. Did you have time for dinner?"

He shakes his head. "I squeezed in an hour at the gym."

"We could run through a drive-through." I slide my foot around in my flip-flop. "You shouldn't miss a meal if you're, um, in training."

He flicks a longer piece of hair off his forehead. "Maybe we can stop at the Eternal Springs Diner on the way home. I heard they're the best in town."

"Where did you get that information? Janney's Place is the best for greasy food." *Not a date. Must introduce him to best friend.* I return to his favorite topic—baseball. "So, were you always a pitcher, or did you play other positions?"

"When I started in tee ball, there were no pitchers. The next year was machine-pitch," he responds. "Then coach-pitch. I played everywhere but catcher. I hated catching." His expression sours and I start to miss his smile. I'm already hung up on his new look. "My dad suggested I try pitching. Coach thought I was pretty good at it and penciled me in as a starter."

Okay...I have nowhere to go with this conversation. "Cool. Um, I played softball for a few seasons."

A smile tugs at his lips, setting off a mini-earthquake inside me. "What position did you play?"

I struggle to remember. "I'm not sure. I remember standing in the grass, counting dandelions. Once in a while, a ball would roll by."

"You were in the outfield," he says. "Probably not center. Left or right."

"One of those, I think. Now I play club tennis."

He cracks up. Seriously. He's dying laughing. And the mini-earthquake inside me hits a ten on the Richter scale.

"You beat poor innocent tennis balls with a club?"

"What? No! I mean, I don't play on the tennis team at school. I play for the Spring River Tennis Club."

His nose wrinkles. "Club tennis. Sounds like fun."

"It's extremely fun," I insist, adding a defensive edge in my voice. "Turn left here."

For the rest of the ride, I let him focus on driving while I use my phone to navigate. Maybe this party will be good for him. Help him meet new friends. Moving to a new school for senior year must be hard.

The address Callie gave me belongs to a house at the end of a crowded street, in one of the newer subdivisions north of town. Two long tire ruts scar the front lawn, pointing the way to the party like freshly drawn arrows.

"Should we knock?" Braeden looks at me like I'm the expert party-goer.

"Better to go around back." I head for the gate and unlatch the lock. The fenced-in yard is wall-to-wall partiers, some from Holy Family, other faces I recognize as alumni, and a few I've never seen before.

"Let's find my friend Callie. I think you'd really like her," I say to Braeden. When he doesn't respond, I glance over my shoulder and realize he's trapped behind a blockade of people, including Mandy and Sophia. What can they possibly be talking to him about? Does everyone in the world already know about his supersonic pitching abilities?

Introductions are exchanged and Braeden's usually quiet mood reverses faster than a lightning strike. He's talking up a storm, like a Braeden I've never met. He might as well be alien Braeden. I'm further astounded when three or four people call his name—before mine.

"Dalisay! You're brave, crossing enemy lines." Tod Bertram, Holy Family's starting third baseman, steps around Mandy to confront my guest.

"I moved here to help you losers finally win a championship," Braeden says, thumping Tod on the back. "I'm transferring to Holy Family for senior year."

Excitement hums through the crowd as everyone gathers to welcome Braeden. Needless to say, I'm happy, too. Braeden has fulfilled my wildest dream by taking all the attention away from me. It's like I'm invisible. Boringly normal. A slow smile creeps across my face.

Leaving him to talk baseball with the Holy Family guys, I practically skip away in search of Callie. Eventually I find her with the youth group gang, hanging out near a portable tiki bar. She's perched on a lounge chair between two unfamiliar guys, talking and laughing.

"Leanne!" Callie jumps up and throws her arms around me. "Hey, Leanne's here!"

The taller guy with wispy blond hair smiles and sticks out his hand to shake mine.

"Miracle girl. I'm Jake." He pumps my arm with serious force.

"And this is Gavin," Callie croons. Gavin's on the short side, about Callie's height, with auburn hair and bright blue eyes.

He nods at me. "Nice to meet you, miracle girl."

"Gavin and Jake go to Spring River High. They work at my day camp as the sports co-directors," Callie says, thrilled beyond belief that she's attracted guys outside of our small high school.

Gavin slings his arm around her shoulders. "Callie's our best junior counselor. She loves those kids."

"Eh, I just give them extra free time so they all think I'm the greatest," Callie says, deflecting his compliment. I want to ask her about work, but she's consumed with all things Gavin and barely wastes a second to look my way.

"Do you swim?" Jake asks.

"Not well enough to be a lifeguard, but I manage," I say.

"This pool is small," he says, breaking away from our friends.

With a final glance over my shoulder, I follow him. Callie's peeking in Braeden's direction while listening to Gavin.

Meanwhile, Jake is still talking about swimming. "I hate working my way into cold water. Better to jump right in, am I right?"

"Sure, I guess..." I'm still watching Callie sneak looks at Braeden, not really paying attention when Jake lifts me off my feet and drops me in the pool. I shriek as I sink into the cold water, deep enough to submerge my whole body before my feet hit the bottom. I blow out a stream of air bubbles, recovering from the icy shock before pushing up to the surface, where I'm greeted by the sounds of laughter and applause.

Jake cups a hand on the side of his mouth. "Check it out, everyone. The pool is now filled with Holy Water." He cannonballs in, drenching me all over again.

Callie peels herself away from Gavin and runs toward us, hanging her toes over the water. "Jake! You did *not* just throw my friend in the pool!" One of my flip-flops floats close to her, and she bends down to grab it. A few other people jump in, as if my dunking signals the party's on. I tread water with fierce kicks, hiding my mixture of rage and embarrassment as the heavy fabric of my cover-up fans out around me.

"Aw, we're just having fun." Jake looks at me. "Right, Leanne?"

"I wasn't ready," I say. "That was rude."

I dive under again, hiding my teary eyes while searching for my missing flip-flop. The bright colors in my new cover-up bleed into the chlorinated water. When I break the surface and rub my eyes, black mascara droplets appear on my hands.

I'm stuck in a cold pool with a wet cover-up stuck to my skin, entertaining a guy I barely know. And worse, Callie deserts me, leaving my flip-flop next to the diving board before disappearing with Gavin. Or Braeden. Oh, shoot, Braeden. Where is he?

Jake snags my other flip-flop before it's sucked into the filter and tosses it on the pool deck, nearly hitting Braeden's shin. Braeden pauses and turns, his dark hair backlit by the paper lanterns dangling from the tree branches. Our eyes meet and I quickly look away. Mandy Stewert calls Braeden's name and he turns in her direction, leaving me with Jake.

I paddle to the edge and hike my body out of the pool.

"Hey, don't go. I'm sorry if I upset you. Are we finished already?" Jake asks, swimming after me. I yank off my cover up and shove it inside my sling bag. Water streams from my hair, dripping on the deck. Shivering, I wrap my towel around me and find an empty chair in the corner of the yard. Hiding in the fringes of the party, I keep an eye on Braeden as he continues to circulate, talking and laughing with a group of the Holy Family athletes. Sophia and Mandy take turns sitting beside him, entertaining him within their tight-knit group. If Callie's interested in him, she's got competition.

"So, are you and Dalisay together?" Jake shakes water from his hair, then lowers himself on the chair next to mine.

I tear my eyes away from Braeden. "You know him?"

"He's the state's best chance for a major leaguer." Jake casually slings his arm over the back of my chair. I lean forward and fake a yawn, trying to add more space between us. He raises an eyebrow, but drops his arm away, finally getting my not-so-subtle message. "We play in the same summer league. I'm 3 for 4 against him this year, so he pretty much hates me."

"Really? You play baseball?" Jake's not as bulked up as Braeden, but he's tall with an impressive reach. Quick, too, judging by the way he tossed me in the pool.

"And varsity soccer. So what about you and Dalisay? You have a thing going or not?"

"Braeden? We hardly know each other. He's my neighbor and offered to give me a ride tonight."

"Hey, Leanne, is it okay if I take off?" Braeden's voice startles me. Ten seconds ago, I'd swear he was wrapped up in conversation with Callie's field hockey friends and now he's right beside me, with Mandy's arm hooked through his. "Do you have a ride home?" He jerks his chin in Jake's direction.

"I'm sure I can find one." But I'd take a silent ride with Braeden over any worthless conversation with Jake.

As soon as Braeden and Mandy disappear, I remember our plan to go to the diner after the party. My stomach starts to burn with emptiness. I'm hungry because I was too nervous to eat dinner. Also, I'm missing time with Braeden. I didn't realize how much I'd been looking forward to it until it was taken away from me.

Jake shifts his chair closer to mine and asks if I remember anything about my miracle. Not in the mood to divulge, I tick off a list of general facts: dates, times, and Vatican procedures. Eventually, he seems to lose interest, especially when I tell him any rumors of my supposed mystical abilities are completely false.

When Jake makes an excuse and heads off to talk to one of his friends who just walked into the party, I hunt down Callie and ask her to take me home.

I feel like I owe Braeden an apology, though I'm not exactly sure why.

~

"Why didn't you tell me about your date with Braeden?" Mom asks, appearing instantly when I press through the side door.

"It wasn't a date, just a last-minute thing. He overheard me talking to Callie about the swim party and offered to give me a ride."

"You two seem to get along well." When I shoot Mom a

look, she quickly adds, "According to Dad."

"Dad has no idea what the rest of us do at work. As long as our jobs get done, he doesn't need to leave his office." I slide out of my flip-flops, dropping them on the tile floor in the laundry room. "Tonight was different. Not work-related." I grab a clean towel from the stack on top of the dryer before heading upstairs to rinse the chlorine out of my hair.

Mom hangs in the doorway, preventing my escape. "I think it's nice that you two are friends. You see a lot of him at work and you were at his house the other day."

I need to correct her false assumption. "I was visiting Sami. Not Braeden."

"You can talk to him, Leanne. I'm not upset about this...boyfriend situation. He seems very responsible."

Right. At least he checked in with me before leaving the party with another girl. "He's not my boyfriend. He drove Mandy home. And you didn't need to tell him about not letting me drive alone with boys, Mom. It was a bit of an overkill and I'm sure Dad told you Braeden drives me to work."

Mom's eyes widen, but she doesn't deny knowing about my daily carpool. We both know tonight was a test and by showing respect for my mother, Braeden passed. I wonder how Jake would have reacted.

Still, no sense getting Mom all worked up about the possibility of something happening between me and Braeden. "He was nice enough to give me a ride to the party, but I don't think he likes me very much at all."

The amazement on my mother's face is priceless. "How could he not like you?"

Oh, let me count the ways. I acted like an ungrateful brat about my miracle. I ignore him at work. He might have overheard me telling Jake that we're just neighbors and now

Braeden probably thinks I don't even want to be friends. But we're not really friends, are we? I mean, we hardly talk. Most days, we barely look at each other.

Suddenly, I'm very tired.

Chapter 12

After the way Braeden left the party, I plan on walking myself to work the next morning. But, when I step outside, he's waiting in his usual spot at the end of the driveway.

I take my time getting settled in his car, avoiding his quiet stare. "You didn't have to pick me up," I say in a low voice.

He shrugs. "We're neighbors. It makes sense to carpool."

Did I imagine a slight emphasis on the word neighbors?

"Reasonable, I guess." I tug on my mint green pleated skirt which is now riding up way too high for my liking, wondering if I should say something about him leaving with Mandy. If anything happened between them, I'm sure I'll hear about it sooner or later from Callie.

Braeden checks the rearview mirror before looping around toward Main Street. "Did you make it home okay?"

"My friend Callie dropped me off. She's the gorgeous blond field hockey star. Did you meet her?" There. I finally said something. Callie can't blame me for not trying to fix her up.

"Was she hanging all over that Gavin dude?"

I press my fingertips into my temples. Callie's infatuation with her coworker might've ruined her best chance to attract Braeden's attention—in a good way. I didn't spend a lot of time with Gavin, but based on my first impression of his friend Jake, I hope my friend chose the right guy to spend time with last night.

Before I come up with a way to leave Callie's options open, Braeden adds, "That Jake guy's a jerk."

And I suspect Braeden knows Jake's feelings toward him are mutual. When I turn to glance at my carpool partner, he's gripping the steering wheel so hard I'm surprised it hasn't separated from the dashboard. No sign of the smile I'd glimpsed yesterday.

"I just met him last night." I could add that nothing happened with Jake, though Braeden seemed so wrapped up in Mandy, he probably doesn't care about that. And if I agree with Braeden, I might seem disloyal to Callie, who brought Jake to the party.

Braeden removes one hand from the wheel and slides it over his jaw. "He cheats at baseball."

"I don't know the official rules, but it seems like cheating would be hard with so many players on the field." I stretch my legs in front of me, wondering how my skirt has magically shrunk since the last time I wore it. Maybe Dad moved some of our wet laundry into the dryer again.

Braeden runs a hand through his hair, further disheveling his already haphazard style. "He argues calls. Cries foul when it's fair. Talks trash on the field to distract the other team. That sort of thing."

I snort. "He also tosses unsuspecting girls into swimming pools."

Braeden's eyes flick to me. "Unsuspecting? You didn't

seem mad about it."

My hand shoots out to grip the door handle. "Really? I must be a great actress, because inside, I was boiling."

Braeden looks skeptical. "What stopped you from telling him off?"

"According to Callie, his dad is an architect and he designed the shrine. I had to be polite." I pause and slide my eyes to Braeden. "Actually, I was hoping you'd help get me away from him. But it seemed like you wanted to take Mandy home—"

"Didn't know you wanted to get away," he says, cutting me off. "I must have misunderstood when I heard you telling him we hardly knew each other."

Ah, so he did hear that part of the conversation. "Because I didn't want him to think we're together...like that."

"Because you like him?"

"No, because even if we were together, it's not any of his business. Besides, I don't date."

Braeden's shoulders ease down into a more relaxed position. "Oh, yeah, I forgot. The dating moratorium."

"A temporary moratorium."

"If it's a temporary moratorium, when do you plan on lifting it?"

I bite my lip, holding my frustration in check. "Can we please stop saying moratorium?"

A hint of a grin spreads across Braeden's face. "You want to place a moratorium on the word moratorium?"

I sigh and press the heels of my hand against my forehead. "You do realize it's incredibly difficult to carry on a conversation with you, right?"

We drive for a block or two. Braeden flips the radio on for half a song, changes the station twice, then turns the music off again. "Leanne, will you please tell me why you don't date?"

"It's a long story," I say, not in the mood to bring up the whole miracle thing around him again. "But I'm sorry if you thought I ditched you last night. I was sad about missing your first experience at the Eternal Springs Diner, even if their burgers are awful."

A smile tugs at his lips. "If you're just using me for a free meal, I'll buy you lunch."

"No, that's not what I meant!" A burst of laughter escapes me. "I probably owe you lunch for driving me every day."

"Darn right you do. And dragging me to a pool party...what was that? The Holy Family crowd's idea of fun?"

"Oh, please. You didn't look too upset surrounded by the Girlfriends."

"The who? Is that like a new band?"

"No, just Mandy's group of friends. The pretty girls who get most of the attention from guys. I'm sure your old school has their own version."

"Interesting," Braeden says. "But no. My old school was guys only. Single-sex education."

"That's still a thing?"

"Yeah, but St. Martha's was our sister school." He arches an eyebrow. "Those girls didn't believe in dating moratoriums."

I give his shoulder a gentle shove. "Would you please be quiet?"

He moves his hand over his mouth, pretending to zip his lips.

"Thank you," I say.

He laughs and the happy sound warms a small, empty space inside me.

"You definitely owe me a meal for abandoning me with

Jake." I fold my arms across my chest, feeling the weight of my dare.

"What did you want me to do? Pull you out of his arms?"

"I wasn't *in* his arms. Like I said, I was trying to be polite."

We sit through a traffic light in silence.

"So, what do you think? Want to sneak out for lunch to-day?" he asks.

But even the thought of going out to lunch with Braeden sets off an alarm in my head. It's too close to my personal def-inition of a date.

"Let's see what's happening at work first," I say. "My dad might need our help with some legal emergency."

He nods. "Sami told me to ask if you're free tonight. She wants to talk about books or something like that."

Ah, so that's why he's playing nice. He wants me to hang out with his sister. Nothing more, nothing less.

"Sure, I can stop by. I have books for her."

Braeden's quiet for a minute, and then says in a subdued voice, "Thanks, Leanne. She looks forward to your visits. It helps her forget the bad stuff... for a while."

~

Dad never comes through with an afternoon deadline, or an-ything to interfere with lunch time, but he assigns Braeden a batch of case summaries and asks me to help Celeste with fil-ing. The phones are quiet through the morning, killing my hopes of a last-minute paperwork request.

Around noon, I'm scanning documents behind Celeste's desk when Mia scoots out of her office. "Who wants to order in? I'm craving a grilled chicken salad from The Green Fac-tory."

I hold my breath. Mia's offering Braeden an easy solution

to the problem of me.

"Celeste?"

Celeste holds up her lunch bag. "Leftovers."

"Braeden?"

He passes a hand over his stomach. "I need more than a salad."

Mia slides open Celeste's desk drawer filled with menus. "They might have a club sandwich on the menu."

"Pass. I'm thinking about going out, though. Want to come?"

I continue holding my breath. By this point, my lips must be turning blue.

With a sigh, Mia spins on her high heels and heads back to her office. "I'd love to, but I'm helping Jason with case prep." She's the only person in the office who addresses Dad by his first name. Even Celeste calls him Mr. Strong.

"Hey, what about you, Leanne? Feel like going out and grabbing a bite?" Braeden shoots me an innocent look and I nearly burst out laughing.

I set down the stack of documents in my hand and grab my purse from the file room, unzipping it to check my wallet before returning to the reception area. "Sorry, I can't do lunch. I don't have any money with me."

He coughs, smothering what sounds like a laugh. "You really want me to buy you food, don't you?"

"No! Wait here. I'll ask Dad for a payday advance."

As I step around him, Braeden touches my arm. "Can you not ask your dad about this? I invited you to lunch, and he'll think I'm a jerk if I make you pay."

"Okay. I'll pay you back, though."

"You can, but I'm not waiting around for that."

"No, really! I promise."

When we pass Celeste's desk, she's chattering away on the phone. She waves to me without lifting her eyes from her message pad. But I hear the smile in her voice.

~

Hungry office workers crowd the narrow streets around the court house, lining up in front of food trucks while checking their phones for the mid-day news updates. The sugary aroma of funnel cake competes with the scent of grilled hot dogs clouding around the town square.

"Where to?" Braeden shoves his hands in the pockets of his khaki pants. "Remember, we're on a budget. I only have twenty bucks."

"No salad?" I ask, reminding him of his conversation with Mia.

"No salad. No sandwiches with strange names. And no fast food."

"You just eliminated ninety percent of our options." I glance down a side street. "Do you like noodles?"

"If the noodle place has air conditioning, I do."

Based on the short line and awesome air conditioner, we decide on Pho Bistro. Braeden pays for two bowls of Pho Cha, which we carry to a table near the window.

While I struggle with chopsticks, Braeden is more adept, making quick work of his lunch.

"Even though it's hot outside, this was a good choice," he says, sucking the final noodle in his mouth as I look on, somewhat horrified. "What? I like soup. That a problem?"

"Not really," I shrug. "You're a slurper. It's actually kind of...um, entertaining." I almost slip and say cute. "Do you miss your old friends?" When he doesn't immediately answer, I continue. "I can't imagine switching schools for senior year.

After you've spent all that time with the same people—"

"I don't miss them. I play with the guys in summer leagues."

"Did you ever have a serious girlfriend?"

He stretches his legs under the table and tugs at his shirt. Even in the air conditioning, he feels the heat. "I was with someone for almost a year, but last summer...we took a break."

"And you're still on a break?"

He smiles to himself. "Yeah. I guess that makes it permanent, huh? Anyway, Sami's starting high school, and it was a good time to move...for her." He pauses and his jaw moves side to side. "Ready to go?"

Outside, we're only two steps away from air conditioning before I miss it. My legs feel heavy from the heat. "Ugh. It's too hot to work. Do you think anyone would miss us?"

He pauses, and some inner debate appears to rage in his head. Sliding his hand over mine, he tugs me in the opposite direction. "Come on. We still have time."

His grip is light, like he's giving me the option to slip away, but I don't. Although it's the first time he's touched me like this, it feels strangely normal. We continue for another block, our fingers laced together and I try not to wonder if he held Mandy's hand last night. Or kissed her.

We stop at a playground in a small park. Guiding me around the tall slides and monkey bars, he pauses in front of the swing set. "Let's go for a ride. I'll push."

I hang back. "I'm not a huge fan of swings."

"What? Who doesn't like to swing?"

"Those of us prone to motion sickness." I place a hand over my stomach.

He lifts his eyes to the sky. "And you say I'm difficult.

C'mon, I'll go easy on you."

When I start to wrench my sweaty palm away, his grip turns to granite.

"I promise I won't let you get sick. Take your pick."

I choose the lowest of the three swings and he laughs. The deep, rich sound turns my knees to warm jelly. I can't get enough of this pure happiness coming from him, maybe because it's such a rare sighting. I should record a video on my phone so I can play it back later.

I wrap my fingers around the ropes, testing their strength before lowering myself onto the curved seat, feeling the sun-warmed rubber through my thin skirt. "Go slow, okay? You don't want to clean up if I lose my lunch."

He taps me lightly on the back and the swing moves forward. "Pump your legs. Don't you know how to swing?"

"I'm wearing a skirt," I argue. And it's way too short for the playground. But to keep him happy, I flutter my legs and soar higher. When I lean back, my toes point toward the clouds.

"You got it. Keep going." Braeden pushes me with gentle force, encouraging me to reach higher.

After five minutes of swinging between the sky and the earth, I stretch my legs and gently brake with my flip flops. "That was fun."

"And no lunch lost. Ready to go back to work?" We share a look, each daring the other to suggest we disappear for the rest of the day.

Unable to come up with another excuse, I hop off the swing. "I'm afraid to say no. Otherwise, you might suggest we try zip lining down Main Street."

~

The afternoon floats by with only the hum of the copier to keep me company. My lunch with Braeden already seems distant and surreal, like it happened years ago, not hours. Mia leaves the office first, claiming she needs to study for her summer class. I haul my stack of paperwork into the conference room to set up tomorrow's work. Dad refuses to shred official client communications after scanning, so I slip signed copies of his letters into case folders.

When I turn the corner, Braeden's heading my way. "Ready when you are," he says.

We leave together after wishing a grinning Celeste good night. I'll definitely hear her thoughts about my friendship with Braeden soon.

"Sami texted me this afternoon and I told her I might stop by," I say to Braeden when we turn onto Chestnut Street. "Can you drop me off at my house so I can grab some books?"

At home, I dash up the steps to my bedroom and load my sling bag with six novels and the case where I keep hair cutting scissors. After checking in with Mom, I carry everything over to the Dalisays'. Still dressed in work clothes, Braeden's on the driveway with his ball and glove, pitching to his net. I pause to watch the way his body flows from an opening stance to the actual pitch.

"Do you squeeze in practice before practice?"

The ball hits his glove with the usual thwack. "Every chance I get." He drops the ball and jogs up the walkway to the open front door.

"Sami! Leanne's here!" he hollers.

Mrs. Dalisay appears, rushing out of the kitchen and wiping her hands with a dish towel. "She's not home, Braeden," she says. "Dad took her to the cemetery. She had a rough day."

His eyebrows pop up. "What happened?"

Mrs. Dalisay sighs. "It's nothing earth-shattering, but Gabby called. She decided not to go back to camp this summer. Sami talked to a few of the other girls in her bunk and apparently, they aren't interested in going back either. It seems as if everyone feels they've moved on."

Braeden's expression tightens. "Dad didn't need to leave work early. I would have taken her."

Mrs. Dalisay smiles at her son, though her eyes are wet with tears. "I know you would have taken her, but Dad wanted to do it."

Braeden glances my way and Mrs. Dalisay smiles sadly at me. All of a sudden, I realize I'm intruding on a private family moment. I hold my stack of books out to Mrs. Dalisay. "These are for Sami. Can you tell her that I stopped by?"

"Thank you, Leanne. I'm sure she'll call when she gets home," Mrs. Dalisay says, taking the books from me.

Braeden follows me out of the house, retrieves his ball and starts to throw again. His eyes narrow as he focuses on the square of tape in the center of the net.

"Are you okay?" I ask. Because, it occurs to me, if Sami is hurting, Braeden must hurt just as much.

The ball sails to the net and returns to his glove. "I'm good. See you tomorrow?"

With that, I'm dismissed.

I cross over to my side of the street. In my house, I drop my sling bag on a chair, heading toward the small table set up in the living room. I pick up one of my baby photos, running my fingers over the frame, thinking about what could have been, if I'd needed surgeries on my spine. If they hadn't worked as well as the doctors hoped. How would I have endured it?

I wonder how Braeden endures. He rarely talks about Emeline; never once has he said her name in front of me. My eyes burn and for the first time in a long time, I'm overwhelmed by thoughts of what could have been my life, and I wonder why I was given a way out of something so challenging, while so many other people in the world suffer through something that seems so much worse.

Chapter 13

"How's Sami?" I ask Braeden when I duck in his car the next morning.

He hesitates before feeding me information. "Better. She liked the books."

How are you? I want to ask, but the way he curls his body over the steering wheel, like he's protecting an open wound in his chest, holds me back. I give him silence. I can't ignore the hurt on his face and pretend everything is okay.

At work, I flip out my key to open the office. Dad and Mia are in court and Celeste scheduled an early morning doctor's appointment for her daughter. After switching on the copier, I add water to the coffee machine and scrounge around for filing to keep busy. Celeste usually leaves a to-do list when she's out. Today, nothing. When the phone rings, I rush to pick it up.

"This is Father Foley, the chaplain at the Saint Piera Holy Shrine. I'm calling for Attorney Strong."

"Mr. Strong is in court today. Can I take a message, Father?" I root around in the desk for a pen.

"Actually, I'm calling about his daughter, Leanne. We'd still like her to attend the dedication and possibly say a few words about her miracle. We're expecting quite a large crowd, plus several television crews."

My hand shakes as I scribble a short note for Dad and promise to relay the message. After hanging up, I press my fingers to my forehead, willing my heart to stop pounding. How can I stand in front of a shrine filled with people and pretend to understand what happened to me? I'm not a good example for the deeply religious. I'm a total fraud. The real Leanne is not a highly spiritual person. I try to be a good person, but I'll never rise to the level of what's expected of me. I don't read the Bible for daily inspiration. I read Teen Vogue. Or romance novels.

I struggle to take a breath. The air in the office feels too thin.

"Are you okay?" Braeden's voice startles me.

"I can't do this," I say, more to myself.

He rounds the corner of the desk, striding toward me, his dark eyebrows pulled together. "Can't do what?"

"Someone named Father Foley called. He's the priest at the new shrine and he wants me to talk about the miracle during the dedication. In front of thousands of people, including television crews." I hold up the message with Father's number, wishing I'd let the phone go to voicemail.

Braeden lowers himself into Celeste's chair and waits. I start to pace circles around him.

"The problem is, I have nothing to say. Whenever I try to put the experience into words, my mind freezes. With a huge crowd watching, I'll probably pass out cold on the marble floor."

Braeden sinks farther back into the chair, thinking. "You

can work up to public speaking. Write everything down in case your mind wipes out on you. Start out by practicing in front of me and Sami."

I shake my head. "It's not about public speaking."

"What's it about, then? If you need speech ideas, I can help. Talk about how different your life would have been. If you were..."

If I had trouble walking. Or lived with pain on a daily basis. We both think it, but neither of us says it aloud. I'm fine, with nothing to complain about, while Braeden's family has suffered a greater loss.

"You must hate me." The words pour out from the depths of my guilt-ridden heart.

"I don't hate you, Leanne. The only person I hate is myself." The hitch in his voice is more powerful than the actual words.

I pause my pacing and return my eyes to his. "Why? You didn't do anything to...Emeline." When I say her name, Braeden flinches.

"No, not directly." He rubs the side of his clenched jaw. "But if I'd bothered to pay attention to her, she might not have spent hours sloshing around in a contaminated stream, collecting baby frogs for her science fair project. Instead, I spent the day practicing my curve ball. Worried about the playoffs, not helping my sister." His chest moves when he takes an exaggerated breath. "The next morning, when she said she felt hot, I didn't call my parents at work. She's just a little sick, I thought. Everyone gets sick." A breath of bitter laughter escapes him. "I told her to take a nap and sleep it off."

"I'm sure it was just—"

With a wave of his hand, Braeden cuts me off. "By the time my mom came home that night, Em...she was running a high fever. My parents took her to the hospital. She never came home." His voice cracks. "The doctors couldn't give us an explanation...they don't know why she got so sick so fast."

I bow my head. *No. Medical. Explanation.* How many times had I heard those words from doctors trying to describe what happened to me? But it never once struck me that the same phrase could apply to something else...something much worse.

Braeden's left eye begins to twitch. Suddenly, I feel like I'm gazing through a magic mirror revealing the true amount of hurt he carries with him. It's like hurling my body over a cliff, diving headfirst into the valley of his sorrow.

When a tear slips from his eye, something breaks inside of me. I go to him, wrapping my arms around his neck, letting him rest his head against my shoulder. When his breaths come out harder and faster, I tighten my hold.

"It wasn't your fault," I say.

"Leanne." He breathes my name. "I wish I could go back and change everything. She was always healthy. Constantly moving, laughing. She was alive."

"It's not your fault," I repeat, because I sense that he needs to hear the words.

Braeden eases away and runs a hand over his face. "When your mom talked about your miracle, I was angry. Not at you exactly, but...it bothered me, after what happened to Em. So, I looked into your miracle and read some articles online. There was one doctor who claimed you were misdiagnosed."

"Dr. Wagner labeled me as a fluke. He's probably still looking for alternative answers. But, according to forty other physicians and a slew of Vatican experts, I wasn't misdiagnosed. The validation process for miracles is incredible."

Pushing to his feet, Braeden shoves his hands in his pockets. "But you don't believe it yourself, do you?"

There's the question. The one I knew in my heart I'd eventually need to answer. Strange that in all these years, Braeden Dalisay is the first person to say the words out loud.

"I believe something happened to me that night. And I believe that a least part of it was faith-related." Though I see pain in his eyes, I continue. "It's too much of a coincidence to ignore. The relic was in my house. My mother held it and prayed. She put her faith in someone else...in something else, besides traditional medicine. And maybe that's what scares me the most. I don't know why it happened to me. I feel unworthy—like I need to repay the world for my good fortune." I breathe out a short laugh. "But how do I do that? Where do I start? It's overwhelming."

Out on the street, tires screech and a driver honks their horn.

Braeden rubs at his eyes. "I'm not saying you didn't deserve a miracle, Leanne. But my sister deserved one, too. I still miss her every day."

Our eyes meet and hold. "I know. You miss her and Sami misses her, although you can't talk about her the way Sami does."

The tension in his face eases and he nods. "Sami needs to talk...it helps her in a way it doesn't help me. And you're helping her when you listen to her talk about Em. I'm her brother, and even I can't do that." He reaches for my hand, drawing me close. "Not many people go out of their way to ask about Em. I don't even want to talk to most people about her. But, with you...it's easier. I don't know why, but it is."

"I want you to talk to me," I whisper. "About anything."

"Anything? Does that mean we can talk about that Jake

guy?" His expression relaxes enough that I know he wants to move on...for now.

My lips twitch. "You were right. He's a jerk."

"I don't want to cause trouble if you like him. To be honest, I held back with you because you didn't know the whole story about Em. That's why I left the party."

"That, and Mandy needed a ride," I remind him.

He makes an impatient motion with his hand. "She asked me to take her home. I just dropped her off. Nothing happened."

Since he's being so honest with me, I draw in a breath and admit the truth. "I wish you hadn't left."

"Yeah, you were really mad about it. I was, uh, surprised." He rises from the chair and steps back, eyeing me carefully. "There's something else I need to tell you. A few weeks ago, I said I went to the batting cage with my friend. That night, I also went to see a therapist. I check in with him every couple of weeks."

Acting on impulse, I take his hand and squeeze it in mine. "Thank you for telling me."

"I can tell you a lot of things." A thin light shines from his eyes, one I've never witnessed before now. "You make me laugh."

I flinch. "Why am I so funny?"

"You're not purposely funny, which makes me laugh even more. The first day—June eighth—when you wiped out, running from that reporter, then picked yourself up and told me you weren't a criminal...after you left, I laughed so hard. For like ten minutes."

I wrinkle my nose. "Nice to hear you found my situation so hilarious."

"Hey, I covered for you," he insists. "But I laughed, too.

And when I realized I was laughing, it hurt. Since Em died, laughing always hurts. Every time something good happens, I think about her not being here to see it. It's hard to explain. But with you...it hurts less."

Slowly, he leans in, asking a silent question, giving me the chance to refuse him. I raise my hand to his shoulder and hold him close. Braeden breathes out and I breathe in, filling the air between us with lightness. We share a shy smile.

Below, the door opens and Celeste calls out a hello as she climbs the steps. I spring back, knocking into the desk as Braeden scoots away and disappears into the conference room, pulling the door shut behind him. I slip the message from Father Foley in my pocket. I'll give it to Dad later, after I've made a decision about speaking at the dedication.

~

Dad and Mia return from court with a heavy workload for me and Braeden. The rest of the day passes in a blur of document retrieval, research, and summaries. We order pizza for lunch and the five of us meet around the conference room table. Braeden sits at the opposite end, keeping his distance, which is probably a smart idea. My dad, Mia, and Celeste seem to be overly-interested in what goes on between Braeden and me.

After Celeste releases us from work, Braeden and I walk out together. "You look nice today," he says.

I glance over my wrinkled skirt and blouse with copy machine toner splattered on the front. "Um, thanks. Dressing up is kind of a requirement. But you look nice, too."

He laughs, and the sky above seems to brighten. "Gotta keep the boss happy."

On the short drive home, he reaches for my hand when we stop at traffic lights. His grip is warm and firm, like I'd expect from a pitcher. What I don't expect are the flickers of electricity that accompany his touch, setting my heartbeat off at a gallop. I flip his hand over and study his long fingers woven through mine. "Will you call me later and let me know if Sami wants company?"

"I would if I had your number."

"Your sister has it. We text all the time."

He scoffs. "No way am I asking Sami for your number. She'll find a way to blackmail me over it."

I unzip my purse and pull out my phone. "Give it to me. I'll send you a message."

After weeks of up and down tension between us, phone number negotiations seem like a big step in our friendship.

At home, I breeze by Mom and rush to change into shorts, a tank top, and casual flip flops before my cell starts to buzz.

"Sami wants to know if you're stopping by tonight," Braeden says when I answer.

"Be there in five," I promise.

"I already told her yes. I was supposed to ask you at work and I forgot." After a slight pause, he continues. "She's still...not happy. She asked to go to the shrine."

My fingers fumble over the strap of my sandal. "The Saint Piera shrine? It's not finished yet."

"Leanne's shrine is what she calls it, and she doesn't care. She wants to see it, ready or not. I wanted to warn you."

I circle my bedroom twice, shaking off the tremor of panic in my chest. "Thanks for the warning. I'll think about it."

~

"Thanks for the books, Leanne." Sami is outside, waiting for me in front of her house when I cross the street. "I started reading one of them today."

At her suggestion, we hang out in the backyard, sitting on wicker chairs on the stone patio, facing the woods where I escaped on June eighth.

"So, how are you?" I ask, settling into the flowery fabric of the seat cushion.

She looks past me, into the trees. "Okay, I guess. I'm not going back to camp. It's too hard to start over, without the other girls." She pulls her knees to her chest. "Do you think we could visit the shrine? Braeden said he'd take me to see it, but I want you to go too."

Faced with this specific question, I find it impossible to say no. "Sure. This weekend?"

"I'm free," Sami says.

Music filters out of an open window above us, the same playlist Braeden plays as we drive to work.

I tilt my head back, soaking in the scattered sun rays poking through the trees. "I'm sorry about Gabby backing out on you."

Sami sighs. "It wasn't a huge surprise because she never really liked camp. Her mom made her go. But I wanted to give back, you know? Pay it forward, or whatever. It helped me get through the summer and I thought...maybe I could help someone else." She uncurls her legs and kicks them out in front of her. "Mom says everyone grieves differently. She has bad days, when she needs to be alone. Dad works a lot more now."

"When I was a baby, my dad worked a lot, too. He had a job with a big firm, plus he was stressed about all my medical bills. At least, that's what my mom said."

"And Braeden...he's different now. I wish you knew him before. He talked a lot. He was funny, too. He always made everyone laugh."

I bite back a smile. "I don't mind him too much."

Sami rolls her eyes. "You can be honest with me. I can't imagine being stuck in an office with him all day."

"We're busy at work, so I don't see him much. You get him on nights and weekends."

She laughs. "You can have him on the weekends, too. Anytime."

As she plays with her ponytail, I remember my promise to her. "Your hair is really long. Do you still want me to cut it?"

Her eyes shine. "Can you try a Dutch braid, too?"

We set up a makeshift salon, shifting Sami's chair around to capture the movement of light as the sun sets. After I mist her dark hair with my water bottle, I spray a detangler over her long waves. Her shoulders relax and she settles back into the chair while I comb out the knots, then carefully snip the ends, one finger length at a time, the way my aunt taught me. Removing one inch of hair doesn't make a huge difference, but an hour later, once I've straightened the front pieces and twisted her hair into a side Dutch braid, I hand her a mirror and she breaks into a huge smile.

"I look awesome."

I circle around her with the mirror, giving her a complete view. "Beautiful."

"Gorgeous, Sami," Mrs. Dalisay adds, watching through the screen door. "I can work a basic braid, but something that complex isn't in my skill set. Would you like to stay for dinner, Leanne?"

I gather up my brushes and hair scissors. "Thanks, but I should go." I hate leaving my parents alone at meals, though in two years they'll be empty-nesters.

"Sami looks great," Braeden says as he walks me to the door. "You must have some real talent."

"She's a pretty girl." I playfully tug at a lock of his hair. "Grow this out another inch or two and I can do something fun with yours, too."

He smiles, revealing his slightly crooked tooth. "Grab a razor and chop it off."

"Really? I like your hair longer." I can't imagine him with a buzz style.

"It's my summer cut. Maybe not this year, though." Leaning against the doorway, he starts to say something else and stops. After clearing his throat, he continues, in a low voice. "Go out with me later? You can show me more of the Spring River hot spots."

I tilt my head to the side, a smile playing on my lips. "But you'll miss a night of baseball practice."

"Practice was called off. Coach went out of town for the July fourth weekend."

"Oh, right. I completely forgot about the holiday," I say and when he remains silent, I realize he's waiting for an answer. "Sure. Let's go out. After dinner?"

He breaks into a triumphant grin. "What about your moratorium?"

"It was temporary," I remind him. "As of right now, it's been lifted."

Chapter 14

If I'm breaking my moratorium and going on a date with someone, I have to admit Braeden's a good choice. We've spent weeks working and driving to the office together. Tonight feels like taking the next step that was meant to happen for us, but still, I'm beyond nervous.

I rush through a shower and brush every knot from my hair. I haven't had time for a haircut lately, and now my longest layers reach the middle of my back.

Over dinner, I break the news to my parents. They share a look, a cross between 'I told you so' and 'What did we get ourselves into having a teenage daughter?'

"Relax. I'm going out with Braeden," I say. "He lives across the street, goes to church every Sunday and works for Dad."

At the sound of the doorbell, I jump up from the table.

Dad follows me out of the kitchen. "He's here? Already? I need to prepare a list of questions."

"Too late," I call over my shoulder. Thankfully my father

rises to the occasion and takes charge of the Strong family welcoming committee. Better him than my mom's oversharing about her dating rules.

"Hi, Mr. Strong." The strain in Braeden's voice is a small but noticeable change. The guys exchange a few brief sentences including the obligatory legal case discussion that's unavoidable whenever they're together. By the time I reapply lip gloss, they're laughing and shaking hands.

"Have a good time, kids," Dad says, retreating to the kitchen where Mom's probably waiting to interrogate him.

Braeden takes my hand on our way to his car, parked on the street under a shady elm tree. His hair is damp and it looks like he might have made an attempt to tame it. When he leans past me to open the door, I breathe in the scent of his rich-smelling soap.

He slides behind the wheel and shoots me a shy smile. "Where should we go? I still don't know much about Spring River."

In my head, I sketch out a map of the most popular places in town. "Want to try the Summer Creamery? They serve homemade gelato and ice cream, but the lines wrap around the block on summer nights."

He starts up the car. "We've got time. Direct me."

We circle the side streets until we find an empty parking spot. Braeden feeds two quarters into the meter before we set off toward the open air café, sitting between an antiques store and a florist. After sunset, the more expensive restaurants fill with the after-work crowd meeting up to share a late meal or a bottle of wine on an outdoor patio, while the younger kids collect on corners and huddle around the casual cafés and coffee shops.

We wait about twenty minutes, chatting about the local

restaurants until we reach the crisp air conditioning inside The Creamery, which brings out a rash of goose bumps on my skin. I cross my arms over my chest and try to keep from shivering as I spend an obscenely long amount of time picking a flavor. Braeden laughs when I eventually order a vanilla and chocolate twist.

"A hundred and fifty flavors and that's what you pick?"

I lift my chin. "I like my standards."

"Not me. I'd get something new every time. Try them all by the end of the summer."

He orders a double black raspberry, the flavor of the day. A red-haired girl behind the counter hands us two cones and we head outside. The instant a table clears, I rush over and stake my claim on the empty chairs.

"Do you and Callie hang out here?" he asks and I'm sort of surprised he remembers her name.

"Not too much. We like movies. Every summer, we make a list of shows we want to see at the Multiplex."

He drops into the chair beside me and scoots closer. Our elbows bump as we try to contain the fast-melting ice cream. "So, if I want to find Holy Family people, should I go to the movies?"

"Depends on the movie. Most of the cool kids hang out at Moonlight Pizza, after football games in the fall. And parties, once in a while...normal high school stuff, I guess. You'll learn, eventually."

We linger at the table, eating our dessert and people-watching while the twilight air curls around us, gentle and sweet. Braeden asks more questions about Holy Family High and I ask him about baseball. Then, we joke about Mia's cat-themed wardrobe and Celeste's fear of the scanner.

"The other day, when you were delivering documents to

the courthouse, I thought she was going to faint when your father asked her to scan an invoice," Braeden says. "But Celeste is nice. She's like my work-mom, always checking in on me." Melting ice cream drips over his hand and arm, forcing him to shift in his seat.

I rip a bunch of napkins from the dispenser on the table and pass them to him. "Lick from the side. Like this." I demonstrate.

He attempts to copy my method, but the result is an epic fail. Blotting his arm with a napkin, he shoots me a helpless look. "I didn't know there was a secret to gelato."

"No secret." I grab another napkin and hand it over, biting back laughter. "I think you're a lost cause."

When two hungry gulls circle overhead, Braeden gives up and throws the melted mess in the trash.

"Let's take a walk. You can show me around."

We turn down a street lined with shop windows sheltered by green awnings and painted signs hanging over doorways.

"Do you talk to Mia much? Outside of work?" I ask when Braeden pauses to check out the team jerseys in the Spring River Sports display.

His brow furrows. "No. Why would I?"

I purposely keep my voice light. "When we're at work, you talk to her a lot."

"She's cool. Smart, too," he says with a shrug.

"The first thing she did when she met you was calculate your age difference."

He snaps out a laugh. "No way."

I cast a sidelong glance in his direction, wondering if I'm some form of a consolation prize. He pulls his attention away from the storefront and reaches for my hand. At his touch, my heart feels lighter in my chest. Even though on some level

I might have picked up on his more than passing interest, it took until right now for me to really, truly accept that Braeden likes me. I'm actually on a date with him and we're having fun. Not at all like I'd imagined the awkwardness of going out with a guy for the first time.

I wonder why I waited so long to try this.

"Braeden!" An unfamiliar voice calls his name, tearing through the cloud of happiness around us. Braeden startles, then tenses, pressing his front teeth into his lower lip.

A tall girl with honey-colored hair crosses the street, waving her arm wildly. "Hey! I'm so happy we ran into each other. I called Sami and told her I was in Spring River tonight, but she was tired, so I didn't stop by the house."

"Yeah, Sami's had a rough week," Braeden replies flatly.

The girl pauses, her sky blue eyes taking in the tightness in Braeden's expression. "You weren't at the beach last weekend. Did you forget about us?"

Tilting his chin up, he focuses on the brick front of the store across the street. "Baseball tournament. I was too tired to drive to the beach afterward."

She rolls her lips into a pout. "It's only two hours away. You could have made an effort for my birthday, Brae." When his eyes cut in my direction, she finally notices me. For a second, her face freezes in a mask of surprise. She takes a quick breath, then flashes a mega-bright smile. "Sorry to intrude. I'm Harper. Braeden's neighbor."

I force myself to smile back. "I'm Leanne. Also Braeden's neighbor."

Braeden looks like he'd prefer to be anywhere else on the planet.

Harper's laugh has a forced shrillness. "Oh, ha-ha! It's funny to think of the Dalisays living next door to um, other people." She turns her attention back to Braeden. "Do you remember Grace Madrina? She's waitressing at The Wheelhouse, a couple blocks away." Harper points in the general direction of the restaurant. "We're hanging out later, after her shift. Spring River is a cool little town, isn't it? I love the art galleries and boutiques." Without waiting for a reply, she rolls into an update of her seemingly eventful summer. Honestly, though, anything sounds more fun than working in a law office. Eventually, a car rounds the corner, traveling above the speed limit, forcing Harper to pivot away from us. When she runs out of steam to power her ceaseless train of one-sided conversation and reaches out to hug Braeden good-bye, he lets go of my hand to hug her back.

"Don't be a stranger, okay?" She pulls back, concern filling her blue eyes. "Even though we don't see each other every day, you can't just disappear. We all miss you."

Braeden's mouth curves upward into a weak smile. "I know. I miss everyone, too. We'll keep in touch."

With a nod to me, she sets off in the direction of The Wheelhouse. When she's lost in the crowds filling the street, I turn back to a stone-faced Braeden.

"Is she your ex?"

He looks at the ground. "Yeah. That's her."

I give him bonus points for honesty.

"She's very pretty," I say, because I'm not sure what else to talk about.

A streetlight blinks on, burning a dot of yellow into the graying dusk.

"Harper's always been like that," Braeden says, as if he senses my need for an explanation.

"Like what, exactly?" I want to know more, but I don't want to make her into a big deal.

"Self-involved?" Braeden grasps for a better description. "She didn't even ask why Sami was tired. And Sami loved Harper."

"It's strange how you two were neighbors...and now we're neighbors," I muse aloud.

His shoulders raise. "She grew up next door to us. Sami and Em looked up to her, followed her around the neighborhood. But after Em died, everything was different. Harper spends summers at the beach. She came home for the funeral, but she didn't really talk to me or Sami much after that. When school started, we decided to take a break." He blows out a shaky breath. "I needed time to myself, but Sami missed Harper a lot." He stops and turns to me, taking my hand, keeping me from walking away. "When Sami started asking about you, I was worried. She gets attached quickly and takes it hard when people disappoint her."

"Sometimes I don't know what to say to her," I whisper. "Or you. I've never lost someone close to me."

He lifts a shoulder. "There's probably nothing you can say that's right or wrong. But at least you try." Around us, the sounds of traffic and music around us seem to fade, like the town is wishing us good night. Braeden breaks into a small smile. "Just keep feeding her books and fixing her hair."

We laugh, but it's not the same easy laughter we shared before Harper appeared.

When Braeden drops me off in front of my house, he parks on the street, strategically positioning us away from a direct view of my front window.

"Thanks for the ice cream. Next time, my treat," I say, unable to come up with anything more spectacular to end the evening. I grip the door handle as my stomach launches into an Olympic caliber tumbling routine. Will he try to kiss me?

"It was nice to get away from...everything." His eyes flick toward his house and back to me. "Can I kiss you?" he asks, his voice rich and low.

I lean into him, giving him my answer. A waterfall of starlight streams through the windshield as Braeden reaches for me, pulling me close. His dark eyelashes lower just before his mouth finds mine. My heart flutters at the taste of his lips, minty and sweet. Our first kiss is light, a simple touch sending warmth radiating through me. But it carries the promise of so much more.

Chapter 15

Last night, when Braeden walked me to the door, I promised to go with him and Sami to the shrine this morning. I thought I could handle it. But now, I'm not so sure.

I manage to down a few spoonfuls of cereal before my phone pings. Braeden, telling me they're ready to leave.

Outside, the sun bakes our newly tarred street, scorching the bottom of my flip-flops. Steam rises from puddles of rain-water, releasing an oily scent into the humid air. I wave to Mr. Webberly, setting up his grill in the front yard. At the end of the block, two other neighborhood dads string rope across the intersection, preparing for our annual Fourth of July party.

"Ready, Leanne?" Braeden calls when he sees me walking toward him. "My parents want us back before the barbeque."

"Can we watch the fireworks later?" Sami lifts her eyes to the sky. "Where do they set them off?"

"At the high school, but you can see them from my back-yard." I pause with my hand on the top of the open car door, catching Braeden's attention while Sami slides in the back seat. "Do you think we'll be allowed inside the shrine? I don't want to get caught trespassing."

He straightens his shoulders and narrows his eyes. His tough guy look, I suppose. "No way is Leanne Strong getting arrested for trespassing on her own personal shrine."

"It's not my shrine. It's Saint Piera's shrine."

A corner of his mouth lifts. "My bad. Let's give the right person her props for performing miracles."

"Thanks for coming with us," Sami says, when I overcome my flash of fear and bend my body into the car. "Everything's more fun when you're around."

"Hey, I heard that." Braeden crumples up a slip of paper left in the center console and tosses it over his shoulder, aiming for his sister. As we cruise through the deserted downtown, the sky begins to cloud up and I push my sunglasses up to the top of my head. Meanwhile, Braeden argues with Sami over music. She loves dance songs and, according to Braeden, has wasted away the balance of their shared online account.

"What kind of music do you like, Leanne?" Sami asks.

"No boy bands in my car," Braeden warns.

"I like what Sami likes," I say, choosing a side.

He heaves a sigh. "Girls always stick together." As they bicker over radio stations, I steel myself for the first sight of the nearly-completed shrine.

"Everyone must be out of town for the weekend," I say, noting the quiet streets and lack of traffic. Braeden moves one hand off the steering wheel, resting it in the space between us, and I'm tempted to twist my fingers through his. Probably not the best idea with Sami's prying eyes close by. I glance at him and he gives me a small smile before glimpsing in the rear view mirror. He knows what I'm thinking; we'll keep our secret for now.

We turn on Cross Street and the shell of the shrine appears

behind a chain link fence. A clean layer of stucco covers the front façade and the smell of wet cement thickens the air.

Braeden parallel parks in an empty street spot, maneuvering the car between a minivan and an SUV. Sami lowers the back window of the car, taking in the shrine with a wide-eyed stare.

"Ready?" Braeden asks under his breath.

I push the door open and step out of the car. As we travel through the open gates and up the newly-set brick walkway, hammering and sawing noises buzz in my ears. A group of tourists—my assumption due to the abundance of picture-taking going on with phones and digital cameras held high in the air—strolls around, avoiding the work crews. When a women wearing a hard hat and yellow vest notices our approach, she turns and signals to the crew. All construction comes to a halt.

"It's her." A gray-haired man with deep lines in his tanned facelifts his camera and snaps my picture. Another, younger woman whips out a phone and starts filming, while ten additional pairs of eyes turn to me.

Uh-oh.

Braeden speaks out of the side of his mouth. "How do they know you?"

"They always know me," I say. "I must give off a miracle vibe."

The cluster of tourists moves closer and the not-subtle questioning begins.

"Are you here to pray with us?"

"Did you change your hair? I thought you were a blonde."

An older lady pushes her oversized sunglasses up on top of her head, revealing the tears in her eyes. "Oh, Leanne. You're beautiful."

When she reaches out to touch me, I suck in a deep breath. In a blink, the wind seems to pick up, tossing my loose hair and blowing over the hem of my sundress, billowing the white material around my legs. The clouds open up and streaks of sunshine pour down, washing over the shrine.

The woman backs away, her mouth falling open. Another woman makes the sign of the cross and mumbles a prayer under her breath.

Ignoring their reaction, I reach a shaky hand down to smooth out the skirt of my sundress. When I look up again, the clouds have slid back over the sun. The crowd of tourists appears frozen, staring at me.

Braeden gives me a funny look. "Does this happen often?" he asks in a low voice.

With a shrug, I say, "I'm used to it."

Shaking his head, he says, "I don't like the way they're looking at you. Like you're...not real."

Sami whispers my name. "Should we run away?"

I'm afraid to move. Braeden shifts closer to me, assuming a protective stance. "They're still staring. Just smile," he says, through gritted teeth.

Sami's lips quiver as she struggles to remain calm. "This is weird."

"Miss Strong, when did you arrive?" A young priest with clipped brown hair and round glasses breaks through the crowd. He waves everyone off and makes a quick sign of the cross, blessing us all. "Relax, people. It was a summer breeze, not a choir of angels." He bows to the tourists. "Welcome, visitors. Please give Miss Strong some personal space." The hammering and sawing resumes. Cupping his hands around his mouth, the priest continues. "Thank you, construction crew. Don't forget, we're paying you triple time to finish the roof before the bishop arrives."

The priest straightens his glasses before turning to Braeden, Sami, and me. "Quite an entrance, Miss Strong. I'm Father Foley." His hand dwarfs mine when we shake. "I take it your father delivered my message?"

Uh-oh. I remember the crumpled note stuffed in my skirt pocket. I never mentioned it to Dad. Should I lie? Father Foley seems like the kind of priest who understands how hard it is to be perfect. The guy we'd all line up to visit when it's time to go to confession.

"Actually, Father, I spoke to you when you called. And, um, I forgot to give my dad the message. But, I'm here to look around, if that's okay."

His lips curve into a smile. "Ah, a reconnaissance mission. Would you like an unofficial tour?"

I hike my thumb in Braeden and Sami's direction. "Can I bring my friends?"

Father waves them over. "Everyone is welcome. Follow me. We'll start in the narthex."

Braeden and Sami fall in step behind Father Foley and me. After exchanging introductions, the priest leads us into the future shrine. We step into the narthex, an open space with white marble floors and high arches. Light drops in through windowless cutouts, washing over a life-sized statue of Saint Piera holding a baby.

Braeden moves away from us and tugs on the burlap wrapped around the base of the Saint Piera statue. "Still unpacking, Father?"

Father polishes his glasses on his shirt before returning them to his face. "We're receiving new pieces every day. That one was quite a handful."

"Is that your saint, Leanne?" Sami asks.

"Yes, that's her," I answer. And me, I add silently.

Sami turns to Father Foley. "When I was little, my Filipina grandmother would tell me that every time I entered a new church, I could make a wish. Do you think I could do that now, even though you're not quite open for business?"

Father Foley smiles. "By all means. Go right ahead."

Sami bows her head and squeezes her eyes shut. Braeden and I follow her lead, though I'm not sure what to wish for. My mind blanks and I quickly decide to double down on whatever Sami wants.

When I open my eyes again, I notice the in-process mural above the wide glass doors leading into the church. The background paint matches the bright yellow color of my bedroom and I recognize the sketched-out design of my antique crib, presently in storage in our basement.

Witnessing my miracle in this way, watching it unfold before my eyes, shakes me to the core. My eyes begin to burn. All my life, I'd hoped for a flash of recognition, some memory of what happened on that long ago night. I'm the sole witness to a holy event, but I can't begin to explain how it came about. Years ago, a reporter hoping to scoop the miracle story even suggested hypnosis as a way to unlock my subconscious, but my parents refused to make that decision for me. Fifteen years later, I'm left with vague dreams or a glimpse of a scene playing in my mind, never knowing if the picture in my head is close to the reality of a medical miracle or an absolute fabrication.

Standing in the narthex, immersed in light, marble, and glass, I wish I could slow down time just enough to process the emotions swirling inside of me. In the stillness of the open space, I feel the presence of something greater, a power that's both scary and completely blissful at the same time. It's like the answers I'm looking for are dangling in front of me, but I can't touch them or see them. Some other, additional sense is engaged right now, and I don't know how to use it. Is that what faith is? A part of you that you'll never truly understand, something that can brighten or fade, depending on the moment.

"Leanne, are you okay?" Braeden touches my arm.

"I'll get her some water," Father Foley says before disappearing through an open doorway blocked by a curtain.

I take a deep breath. "I'm fine. This place...it's beautiful."

"Yes, it is." Sami steps next to me, pointing to the high wall above the doors. "Did you see the mural? It's almost exactly what I picture in my head when I think of your miracle. The color yellow, and the brightness of the light."

Father Foley returns and hands me a paper cup. I take a sip of water, trying to collect myself. Braeden peers through the glass wall separating the narthex and the church. "No pews yet, Father?"

"Not yet. They have been commissioned, though. And the altar should be arriving soon. It's from St. Piera's home parish in Italy."

"Can I say a prayer for my sister?" Sami asks.

Braeden clears his throat. "We should. Light a candle or something." He turns to Father Foley. "Our sister Emeline...passed away last year."

Father Foley rubs his hands together, like he's performing a pre-worship warm up. "Of course we can pray. We don't need pews for that." The four of us bow our heads and Father recites a quick prayer.

After we say amen, he whips a small pad of paper and pencil from his pocket and carefully scribes the name Emeline Dalisay. "I'll add her to my prayer list for the dedication," he says.

"All I request in return is your attendance."

"We'll be there," Sami says, unaware of my trepidation. Because, really, who would believe that I wouldn't want to attend a celebration of my miracle? "Can we come back again before the dedication? Maybe when the stained glass windows are in?" she asks Father.

"Whenever you wish," he promises. "The three of you have an open invitation."

With a quick glance at me, Braeden takes Sami's arm and leads her away. "Take a look at this fountain, Samster. I've never seen one this huge inside of a church."

Father Foley turns to me. "Will I see you at the dedication?"

I hesitate. "I don't know if I can talk in front of everyone."

Behind his round glasses, Father Foley's green eyes soften. "Do what you can, Leanne. Your presence is more than enough."

Chapter 16

Somewhere between the shrine and Chestnut Street, Sami asks, "Hey, Braeden? Why are you holding Leanne's hand?"

Braeden lifts our joined fingers. "You don't miss a thing, Samster."

Awkward silence.

"So, when were you gonna inform me about this situation?"

Braeden's mouth twitches into a smile. "You need to pay more attention to what's going on around you. Mom and Dad already know. Leanne's parents, too."

More silence. Not quite as awkward, though.

Sami leans out of the back seat, sticking her head between us. "Wait. How long has this been going on?"

I bite my lip to restrain a laugh.

Braeden doesn't bother hiding his amusement. "Doesn't Leanne tell you everything when you have those secret girl talks in the backyard?"

Sami giggles, her brown eyes bouncing between me and her brother. "I must not have asked the right questions. So are you two together?"

Braeden scoffs. "You think I'd just hold anyone's hand?"

"No one since Har—" Sami cuts herself off, but I can easily guess who she's talking about.

Pulling into the driveway, Braeden ignores her slip. "Go inside and tell Mom we're here while I walk Leanne home. We have a few hours to kill before the block party starts."

"It doesn't take a few hours to cross the street," Sami says, laughing as she leaps out of the car and races up the walkway to fill her mother in on our eventful morning.

~

I grab two sodas from the fridge, though it's barely lunch time, and carry them out to the deck, hoping to catch the tail end of the morning shade before the sun peaks over the trees. Braeden and I swing on the glider overlooking the section of the yard filled with blue hydrangeas, their sweet smell floating in the air.

"Do you want to do something?" I ask, worried that he's bored.

"This is something." Braeden slides his arm around my shoulders. "What happened at the shrine? Outside, in front of the crowd. And inside, you were shaking when you saw the mural."

I pull my legs up and tuck them against my chest, letting Braeden propel us back and forth. "I'm not sure." In the sky, only innocent white clouds float above us, making me question my memory of the incident. "I've never been able to picture that night. June eighth. When I saw the statues, the mural, an entire building focusing on one event in my life..." I pause, struggling to find the right words. "It was like something locked inside of me finally opened up."

Braeden leans back and the glider creaks at the shift in weight. "Does it scare you? Is that why you never want to go there?"

"Not scary. Just a lot to take in." We swing for another minute. "Did it scare you?"

"The light and wind? That was wicked cool."

I gnaw on my lower lip. I'd hoped the freaky breeze hadn't been obvious. "If it hadn't been that, something else would have captured their attention. It's like people are looking for miracles when they're near me. They search for any possible sign and overanalyze everything."

Braeden sits up straighter and halts the motion of the glider. He turns to me and I start to lose myself in the deep brown warmth of his eyes. "What do you think it was?"

"A coincidence?" But I hear my voice falter. "I don't know. But I don't want to question every unexplained event, either. I think some things can never be explained."

"I agree." He takes a sip of his soda, staring off into the bushes. "You don't scare me, Leanne."

We swing for a while, with only the creaking movement of the glider breaking our silence. The heat and humidity builds and my skin feels damp.

"Can I watch one of your games?" I ask. "I'd love to see you pitch."

He shoots me a grin. "Only if you bring Sami with you."

"She says your games are boring."

Braeden looks slightly offended. "She's lying. She screams her heart out every time. She's my loudest cheerleader."

"I could be a contender for that title."

The sliding door clicks open. Dad pokes his head out slowly, like he's afraid of walking into something he doesn't want to see. "How's everything going back here?"

I glance over my shoulder. "Fine, Dad. You can come out."

Braeden stands and shakes my dad's hand. "How are you, Mr. Strong?"

"Terrific. A beautiful day, isn't it?" Dad moves around the perimeter of the deck, staying as far from the glider as possible. "Mrs. Strong wants me to roll the grill into the street now. So, we'll be on the other side of the house, talking to the neighbors. And you'll be..." Dad throws me a heavy stare.

"Around front in ten minutes. I promise."

"Got it. See you in ten minutes." Dad grabs the handles of the grill and tips it back to begin the short jaunt through the gate and around the side of the house. "Wouldn't want Braeden to miss his first Chestnut Street block party."

As soon as he disappears, Braeden and I laugh.

"He's completely freaked out," I say.

Braeden chuckles. "If I had doubts about your dating moratorium, they're gone now."

"He needed to face reality some time. It's not like I wasn't ever going to...you know."

"What? This?" Braeden returns to the glider, winds his arms around my waist and lowers his mouth to mine. We soak up our last ten minutes alone with nonstop kissing. It's not a bad way to celebrate Independence Day.

~

The moon bounce swaying in the middle of Chestnut Street practically bursts with toddlers' happy screams.

"Will you hang out with me now, Leanne?" Sami nudges her elbow into Braeden's gut. "She's my friend too, brother."

"I know, Samster. We're all friends."

Her brown eyes dim. "You two are all I've got. I don't know why we moved. I had tons of friends back home and here, there's no one." She hops up on the curb, adding four inches to her height as she walks along beside her brother. "Seriously, this block party stinks. Ours was way better. Remember when Harper's dad paid for the ice cream truck to give out free cones?"

Braeden slings his arm around her narrow shoulders. "I'll buy you ice cream if you miss it so much."

"It's not like living here is so much better. Dad still works. Mom's still tired all the time." She shrugs out of her brother's hold, tears falling from her eyes.

I step sideways, blocking her from a group of younger kids playing kickball in the street while Braeden hugs her into his side, letting her cry.

"We needed to try something," he says in a low voice.

Backing away from him, she fights for a breath. "I know. But it's hard."

I tilt my head and catch Braeden's attention, flashing a silent message, telling to leave her with me. He sets off in the direction of a long buffet table loaded with fruit salads and veggie dips.

Sami sinks into the grass and crosses her legs.

I crouch down next to her. "Can I braid your hair? It's hot today."

She wipes her tears away before reaching in the pocket of her shorts. "I found something new on Instagram and saved the picture on my phone. I want to try double braids, looped together."

I study the picture before running my hand over her glossy waves. "You definitely have enough hair to carry this off." I twist and tug for twenty minutes, waiting for her breaths to slow and giving her time to recover. When Braeden returns, he's carrying two gloves and a baseball.

He drops a glove in Sami's lap. "I need you to catch for me."

She rises with a huff, tossing her braids. "This is supposed to be a non-baseball day."

He tosses the ball in the air and catches it behind his back. "There's no such thing as a non-baseball day."

With his awesome aim, she only needs to hold the glove out at the correct height. Braeden's throws hit their mark every time; he's a machine.

When Sami tires of the game, she lobs the baseball back to her brother, tosses the glove my way, and heads over to her parents, sitting in the shade.

"No more baseball. Let's do something else."

He follows me into my garage, where I pick up two tennis rackets and pop the top off of a new can of balls.

He grins. "Club tennis?" Racket in hand, he jogs to the street and lobs the tennis ball to me. We volley back and forth for a while, but Braeden's hits usually sail over my head.

"This is a friendly game. Stop trying to hit a home run," I yell after picking one of his bombs out of the bushes.

He raises his hands in a helpless gesture. "I like to swing."

"Really? Then chase this." I serve a rocket wide to his right. When he scrambles after it, I find an empty chair and fan my face with my racket.

He returns with the tennis ball and touches his lips to my cheek, right in front of everyone.

"I'm sorry," he says, but I know he's not.

I tap the racket against his chest. "You hit them away from me on purpose."

"Maybe I did," he admits. "I thought you might want a challenge."

"Ugh. It's too hot to run today. No challenge needed."

"Can we watch the fireworks together?"

I search for his sister. "What about Sami?"

"She dumped us tonight. Gabby called and they're friends again. She invited Sami to her house."

When our neighbors begin lining chairs along the curb, Braeden and I dash around my house, returning to our seats in the glider. I light a lemon candle and place it on a nearby table to keep the bugs away. The tall trees fade into the darkness as fireworks shoot high above us, bursting between scattered stars. I lean my head into his chest, listening to his heartbeat as we watch the final lights burn out and return the sky to darkness.

He loosens his grip on my hand. "I should go home soon."

"Not yet." I raise my arms and loop them around his neck. This need to be close to him is still so new and I'm determined to hold on to our last few minutes together. I don't want him to leave, if only because he makes everything in the world seem brighter than the fireworks spiraling through the night.

~

By the time Monsignor releases us from church on Sunday, Sami and I have worked out big plans for the afternoon.

Braeden gripes when we insist on riding with him to his game. "If you go with me, you'll have to sit through warm-ups."

Sami huffs. "Warm-ups take forever. Can't you be late for once?"

"Not if I want to start. Be ready in an hour or the team bus leaves without you," he says, tugging her ponytail.

The sports park is a twenty-minute drive from our end of town. Braeden pulls into the gravel lot, tires rolling over weeds sticking up through the stones. As we cross the grass field behind the baseball diamond, traffic hums along the elevated highway running off in the distance.

Braeden slings his long bag over his shoulder, forging ahead, his mind already consumed with the upcoming game. He leaves me with Sami and we pick a spot along the first base side, close enough to offer a clear view of the pitcher's mound.

I spread a blanket on the grass, eyeing Braeden from afar as Sami kicks off her flip-flops and we sit cross-legged while a fat bumblebee buzzes in circles, like it's dizzy from the heat. Waiting for the game to start, my eyelids grow heavy. The rhythmic sound of practice bats cracking against balls lulls me to the edge of sleep.

Sami coughs, startling me. "I'm sweating," she says. "And my head hurts. Why isn't there any shade here?"

"Cause we'd be hitting balls into trees." Braeden appears, returning to check on us after his warm-up routine. Sami raises her hand to shield her eyes from the sun. "Want my sunglasses?" He holds out the pair clipped to his uniform shirt.

"No, they're too big for me," she says.

I pop open the cooler. "Water?"

"Nothing." She scowls, looking so much like her brother that I need to bite back a laugh.

"Gatorade?" Braeden offers. "I'll grab a bottle from the dugout."

"I said nothing. It's just hot." She lifts her chin higher, daring us to say more. Braeden and I exchange a look. He shrugs.

"Are you starting today?" she asks.

"Heck, yeah." He grabs the water bottle from my hand and takes a long swig before swiping his arm across his forehead. "Should be a good game. We're playing the second place team."

"Are you in first place?" I ask.

"Braeden's team's always in first place," Sami says. "He's the best pitcher in the state."

"Says my sister," Braeden adds, while stretching his pitching arm across his chest.

When the visiting team jogs onto the field for batting practice, my stomach takes a nervous dive. Jake Maddaloni walks out of the dugout, swinging a weighted bat over his head, talking to Gavin O'Connor. Callie's Gavin. After glancing at Braeden, who's glaring at Jake, I pull out a visor from my sling bag and shove it on top of my head, hoping Jake doesn't recognize me.

The umpire calls the coaches to the field for starting lineups and Braeden strides back to the dugout without saying good-bye.

"Sheesh. Have a good game," Sami calls after him.

In the first inning, Braeden strikes out every batter. If I thought his warm-up throws were impressive, his actual game speed is blinding. The ball whizzes out of his hand and before I blink, I hear the familiar thwack of his pitch hitting the catcher's mitt. The batters appear to swing on a delay and most of them fail to even make contact. Jake is the third man out when he whiffs on what Sami describes as a high fast ball.

In the bottom of the first, someone taps my shoulder.

"Hey, friend." Callie parks herself on my blanket. "Didn't know you'd be here." Her eyes are puffy, like she's very exhausted or very upset. Or both.

"I should have called." I stumble out an apology. "I didn't know Braeden was pitching against Gavin's team today."

"No big deal." She lifts her arm, waving to Gavin. On the underside of her wrist, I notice a reddish brown C-shaped mark, scabbed around the edges. She nods to Sami. "Is this your new neighbor?"

"This is Sami. Braeden's sister," I say, as if Callie doesn't already know. "What happened?" I point to her wrist.

"Oh, that. I burned myself making breakfast."

I circle my fingers around her sun-freckled arm, right above the mark. "You just did this? It looks old."

"Maybe yesterday. I forget." She moves her hand away.

While Sami's watching her brother, I lean closer to Callie. "I'm worried about you. Every time you I see you lately, you look stressed."

"I'll be okay," she says, picking at the grass. "But thanks."

"Want to camp out at my house for a while?"

She pauses for a beat, then shakes her head. "No. I need to be home."

I stretch my legs out on the blanket, hoping to catch a few rays. Callie was right when she said I'd be jealous of her summer tan. She's usually paler than me, but working outside has given her a summer glow while my skin looks the same as it did on the last day of school.

"So what's going on with Gavin?" I try to sound casual.

Callie slides her sunglasses down. "What's going on with Braeden?"

"Nothing," I say, but she knows me too well.

"Oh, for sure." She pokes my arm. "Why are you here? A sudden interest in the summer leagues?"

"I asked you first." We stare at each other until we break into giggles.

"Braeden *likes* Leanne." Sami joins our conversation. "He admitted it to me last night."

My already hot face warms up several more degrees.

"Oh, he likes her, does he? I guess that's why he wasn't interested in me." Callie places her hand over her heart, adding to her false sense of drama. "Thanks for the scoop, neighbor-friend." Callie smiles sweetly, knowing she won this round of one-upmanship. "And since you asked, I like Gavin. At least I think I do. I'm kind of on the fence." She scans the field, searching for her current love interest. Once she locates him in the visitors' dugout talking to Jake, she swings her attention to the pitcher's mound. "I'd be happy with Braeden, though. He's looking pretty fine in his baseball uniform."

Sami feigns projectile vomiting. "Please. That's my brother you're talking about."

I clamp my mouth shut, though I totally agree with Callie's assessment.

Between innings, a group of girls about Sami's age stroll by our blanket and stop to chat. After years of watching her brother's games, Sami knows a lot of baseball families. The girls ask about Braeden, and she tells them he's working an office job in Spring River this summer.

While Sami tells the girls about her new house, Callie ducks her head and speaks in a low voice. "Have you kissed him yet?"

I don't need to answer. The smile spreading over my face says everything. "Friday night. And yesterday too—more than once. Are you mad at me for not calling you?"

Callie's eyes widen. "No way. I'm extremely happy for you. But I need details—later."

After three perfect innings, Braeden's accuracy slips a bit. He walks the first batter he faces in the fourth inning and gives up a double before recovering to strike out Jake on what Sami identifies as two fastballs and a slider.

"Braeden must really hate Jake. I wonder why?" Callie directs a pointed stare my way.

I hug my knees to my chest. "Why would Braeden care? I only talked to Jake once."

"Oh, fun. Braeden's jealous," Sami says, catching on.

"No, he's not," I insist.

"We'll see," Callie says, trailing off her words with light laughter.

In the eighth inning, things take a turn for the worse. Jake leads off and gets ahead in the count, three balls and one strike. Braeden shakes off a couple of signs from the catcher and kicks up yellow dirt on the pitcher's mound, thinking about his next pitch. After a delay that sends the opposing coach out of the dugout complaining to the umpire, Braeden reaches back and releases the ball.

The pitch is high and outside, close to Jake's chest. To avoid being hit, he leans back and tumbles to the ground, where the brown dirt around home plate covers his clean white uniform. Braeden drops his arms to his sides, watching Jake scramble to his feet.

"What do you think you're doing, Dalisay?" Jake tosses the bat to the ground on his way to the pitcher's mound.

"Stop leaning into the strike zone." A smug smile appears on Braeden's face. "That's for throwing Leanne in the pool, dude."

Sami shoots to her feet. "Oh, no."

Callie gasps. I brace myself for an ugly confrontation.

"No fighting, gentlemen. Take your base, batter," the umpire calls. Ignoring him, Jake lunges forward and throws a running punch at Braeden, hitting him square on the jaw. Braeden snaps his arm back as both benches clear, followed by parents and coaches storming the field, trying to disassemble the tangled pile of players. Somewhere at the bottom, Braeden and Jake are still going at it, screaming at the top of their lungs.

"Mom's gonna kill him," Sami says, shaking her head.

"She hates washing blood off his uniform."

Watching the riot on the field, my stomach churns bile high into my throat. When Braeden rises from the bottom of the heap, he brushes dirt off his uniform before he's hoisted in the air by his teammates and carried off the field. His shirt is streaked with grass and mud stains. He raises his hand and presses it to the side of his face.

When he passes by, riding high on his teammates' shoulders, our eyes meet. Slowly, he removes his cap, and tips it in my direction.

I shoot him a glare.

Meanwhile, Sami laughs. "He's so gone over you, Leanne."

Chapter 17

The umpire calls for the teams to take a timeout and regroup. While Sami listens to Callie go on about her opinions on the best after-school clubs at Holy Family, I take a walk behind the team bench. From the far end of the dugout, I hear the coach lecturing Braeden about intentionally walking a batter without permission. Braeden bows his head, but his muttered apology is missing any trace of remorse. Another player hands him an ice pack and he presses it to his swollen cheek. When the coach heads to the bullpen to call in a reliever, I whisper Braeden's name.

"How bad is it?" I ask.

He turns around, a smile pushing up the ice pack covering his swollen cheek. "It's all good. I don't think I'll need stitches this time."

I loop my fingers through the chain link fence behind the bench. "Want to tell me what just happened?"

"It's called a brushback." He shrugs. "And I might have overestimated the strike zone."

"Yeah, right. Mr. Awesome Control slipped on a pitch."

He leans back into the bench and casts his eyes toward the field. "Anyway, I feel much better now."

I tighten my grip on the metal fence and the chain links around me quiver. "Because you got thrown out of the game? Was that really what you wanted?"

Braeden's eyes cut away from the field, over to me. "He threw you into a pool. Total disrespect."

To be honest, I'm having trouble defending Jake. But, still, what Braeden did wasn't right. I leave him cradling the ice pack against his cheek, his eyes focused on the next batter.

"Your brother's impossible," I complain to Sami, when I return to the blanket.

She laughs hard enough to send her into a coughing fit. "Tell me about it."

I pat her back. "Do you need a drink?"

Another cough. "Must be my allergies. It's hard to breathe out here today."

"Why don't you sit under the pavilion?" I point to the shelter between the field and the parking lot.

She shakes her head, sending her twin braids flying. "No way. I want to see the rest of this game up close and personal."

With shaky relief pitching, Braeden's team gives up three more runs and wins the game by only one run. Callie abandons us to comfort Gavin, who appears very happy to see her and not as bothered by the loss as Jake, who's still spitting threats in Braeden's direction.

"Ready, girls?" Braeden slides an arm around my waist. His hair is damp with sweat, half his face is swollen and his uniform is streaked with dirt.

"I texted Dad and told him you got kicked out of the game," Sami says. "He wants to know how you could intentionally walk someone by accident."

"I decided to change my strategy and forgot to check with Coach," Braeden says drily.

I sling his baseball bag over my shoulder so he can hold the ice pack on his face. In the parking lot, we spy Callie and Gavin acting like two long-lost lovers drowning in a sea of kisses.

Sami's eyes widen. I call Callie's name to let her know she has an audience.

"Let's hang out today," Callie says, after unfastening her mouth from Gavin's. "If you're not busy with...." She tilts her head toward Braeden.

"I need to shower and clean up," he says.

"And Dad's waiting for you. He's probably gonna make you practice pitching without almost hitting people. That could take hours," Sami says.

Braeden kicks some loose gravel with his cleat before lifting his eyes to mine. "Call you later, Leanne."

With a wave, I jump in Callie's car.

Back at my house, we decide to cook mac and cheese for a late lunch.

"Want to tell me what happened to your hand?" I ask.

She studies the blue box like she needs to memorize the two-step instructions. "If I tell you, will you promise to drop the subject?"

"I can't promise that. But I won't tell anyone else unless you say it's okay."

"Good enough," she says with a sigh. "Mom and Dad were fighting again. Dad still hasn't found a job and Mom wants to borrow from our savings. Anyway, they were so involved in their argument, Mom forgot about the pot of tomato sauce on the oven. It bubbled over and caught the flames. I didn't think—just grabbed the handle without a pot holder, then dropped it back on the burner. A spark caught my sleeve and the sauce splashed on my wrist." She meets my gaze with watery eyes. "It really was an accident. I was so unhinged by their yelling. I'm tired of listening to them fight all the time."

"And the scratches on your hand I saw on June eighth? Was that really your cat?"

"Yes, but it was them, too. They started fighting and poor Oscar zoomed by on his way out of the room. I tried to pick him up and he scratched me." Callie rips open the powdered cheese packet and dumps the contents over our lunch. "They're seeing a counselor—again. They're trying to work it out. Mom's switching from part-time to full-time, I think. In case it takes Dad a while to find something."

"And you're stuck in the middle of it," I say, pouring two glasses of milk while Callie dishes out our mac-n-cheese.

Callie sighs. "Two more years. Then I'm leaving for college and never coming back, even if I need to take every student loan available."

After sweating for nearly three hours at the baseball game, we decide to spend the afternoon soaking up the air conditioning and watching old movies. And by old, I mean 1986. Classics like Ferris Bueller, Sixteen Candles and The Breakfast Club. Hours pass without word from Braeden or Sami and I decide it's probably best for me to stay away from the Dalisay house right now.

"You like him a lot," Callie decides after listening to me go on about all things Braeden.

"I don't have much to compare him to, but, yes, I like him. A lot."

"He's good for you." Her eyes drift to my framed magazine cover, hanging on the wall. "Nearly an even match in the famous department. And he doesn't seem intimidated by that gigantic halo circling your head."

"Neither are you," I say.

"Yeah, but I've known you forever. Long before we realized how special you are."

For some reason, her smart comment makes me reach over and hug her. If I'm ever in danger of a bloated ego, Callie is someone I count on to tear me down to size. I need her in my life. And she needs me, though she'll never admit it.

~

Overnight, Braeden's cheek has morphed into a mini purple bowling ball with blotches of yellow and green. Honestly, he's hard to look at, so I just don't, forcing myself to stare out the window while he drives.

"Does it hurt?" I manage to ask.

"Yes. A lot."

"Next time you want to brush someone with your eighty mile-an-hour fastball, maybe you'll think twice about it."

He runs his hand over the bruise. "It's a brushback, not a brush. And I didn't throw it full force—closer to seventy."

I risk a glance at him and wince. "You're impossible."

His cheek puffs out when he smiles. "But you still like me."

When we enter the office, I hear Celeste's voice singing into the phone.

"Celeste is excited. We must have landed a big case. Or we have a visitor," I say to Braeden as we scale the steps to the second floor. Sure enough, Father Foley occupies one of the three chairs in the small waiting area. His eyes crinkle behind his round glasses when he smiles.

"Ah, my friends are here," he says, holding up his hand for a round of high fives.

"Good morning, Father," I respond, trying to remain professional while Braeden slaps his hand against Father's.

"I see you've met my daughter, Leanne," Dad says, strolling out of his office.

"Leanne and I met the on the Fourth of July." Father nods at me. "She visited the shrine with this fine young man and another friend."

"Sami is my sister," Braeden reminds him.

Dad raises his eyebrows at me, but I suddenly find a fascinating brief on Celeste's desk and pick it up, scanning the legalese.

"What happened to your face, Braeden?" Dad asks.

A choking cough escapes my throat. Celeste thumps me on the back.

"Baseball injury, sir."

"Did you catch a ball with your face?" Celeste drawls.

Braeden laughs. "No, I caught someone's fist instead."

Father Foley and Dad laugh too. I press my mouth shut and continue flipping through the brief.

"How can I help you, Father?" Dad turns back to our guest.

Father Foley removes a paper from his pocket and hands it to Dad. "The township sent this letter to the shrine. Apparently, some of the neighbors wish to protest the final design. Now that we've begun to build, they feel it's larger than the original specs and the architectural style doesn't fit well with the surrounding area."

Dad harrumphs and scoffs as he scans the letter. "Of course it looks out of place. The rest of the neighborhood is old and poorly maintained. People don't appreciate modern design at its finest." He gestures further down the hallway.

"Step into my office, Father. I can type up a reply this morning, but we should talk first."

Ten minutes later, Father Foley exits Dad's office, whistling *Let There Be Peace on Earth*. He pauses with his hand on the door knob. "Will you be stopping by the shrine again before the dedication, Leanne? It's changing daily, sometimes hourly."

I bite my lip, considering. "I'm not sure, Father."

"As you wish. Remember, for you, the door is always open." On his way out, he makes the sign of the cross, a farewell blessing. Celeste and I bow our heads.

"He was interesting," Celeste says, after he's gone. "We don't see many priests in the office."

Picking up a stack of letters to file, I say, "I'm not sure if that's good or bad."

Celeste laughs. "Good or bad for you? Hard to say. No one's asking me to stand up and give a speech in front of thousands of people."

~

Dad sends Braeden on a mission to the Spring River Court House's Judicial Library in search of property dispute cases and zoning laws. He's out of the office through the lunch hour, so Celeste, Mia and I eat in the conference room.

"Miss Leanne, how do you like our new employee?" Celeste interrupts my Braeden-centric thoughts as she unwraps her homemade sandwich. Though her question appears innocent, I know Celeste well enough to interpret her true intention. She's asking me if we're secretly dating.

"He's okay," I admit, hoping Dad's office door is closed.

Mia looks up from her bar exam study guide as she munches on her salad. "You like him, Leanne. And he likes you, too."

I can't meet her curious stare, so I pick at my peanut butter crackers. "I didn't start out liking him. Things changed."

"Well, it's about time you liked someone," Celeste says. "You're a beautiful young lady. And he's a handsome gentleman."

I laugh at her description. "Mom says he's nice, Dad thinks he's responsible, Mia says he's not what she expected in an intern, and you describe him as a handsome gentleman."

Mia's dark brown eyes light with amusement. "And you think he's...fill in the blank, please."

I struggle to find a word or phrase, but I can't. "He's Braeden."

Celeste's eyes bulge as she tears off a bite of her sandwich. "The way you're smiling around here lately, I think I need to find a Braeden of my own."

~

Braeden returns to the office with a stack of case dockets and holes himself up in the conference room. An hour later, he crosses the hallway and enters Dad's office with a typed summary in hand.

"Waiting for me?" he asks when he finds me in the copy room, my feet resting on an empty cardboard box, plowing through the e-book version of one of my summer reading assignments on my phone.

"What's going on?" I stuff my phone in my purse and we head for the door.

"Your father asked me to review a copy of the original traffic projection study commissioned by the township. Father Foley said the neighbors are protesting the increasing number of cars and trucks in the area, but your dad thinks it's still within the stated parameters."

"I'm not surprised about the traffic issue," I say. "Based on my June eighth experiences, that is. People travel from all over the country to pray for miracles."

"That day was pretty epic in our neighborhood."

Outside, the steamy humidity has taken up residence in town. Scary clouds gather in the distance, promising another night of thunderstorms.

"Do you think people will come to the shrine expecting more miracles?" I ask.

Braeden reaches past me to open the car door. "Maybe they won't expect a miracle, but they may hope for one. If you believe in God and you believe in miracles, why not?"

"You're right, I guess." I slide in the front seat and stretch my arm over to his side, unlocking his door. "What if the neighbors don't want to deal with crowds?"

"The township already approved the plans. Based on my research, this is out of the neighbors' hands," Braeden says as we turn out of the office parking lot. A boom of thunder in the distance has us both searching the skies. "And ours, too. Your father did what he was asked when he presented the building plans. No one tried to hide anything. So if God decides that the Shrine of Saint Piera is where miracles will happen, then they'll happen. And people will come, no matter how many residents protest."

I can't help but note the change in his attitude since our first conversation about my miracle, when he was so willing to debate the possibility of its existence. "You mean nothing will change? The construction goes on as scheduled?" A tiny part of me still hopes for the dedication to be delayed or cancelled. Why couldn't they wait until the twentieth anniversary, after I left for college?

"The layout was approved. The neighbors can complain and possibly delay construction or negotiate the size down, but your dad will argue that a smaller shrine might make things worse. It might mean larger crowds outside the building, waiting for their turn to pray."

I shrink down in my seat. "This shrine is causing so much trouble and it's only being built in Spring River because of me."

"Don't sound so happy about it."

"I just...I don't want to be hated in my own community. I'll never be able to come home again."

"Not gonna happen. You put Spring River on the map. The town will make truckloads of money from increased tourism." Braeden pauses. "And everyone knows this wasn't really your decision."

He's right, I had nothing to do with the shrine. I was the last person to find out about the plans. So, why am I worried? Even with the slight disruption to my life, I still have so much to be thankful for. "Sorry. I'm acting like a total drama queen again."

He brakes at a traffic light and covers my hand with his. "You never asked to be famous, but you're handling it. That's all you can do."

"Some days, I handle it better than others." On bad days, it's easier to forget how lucky I am. I need to remind myself that I can deal with whatever this shrine will bring to upset my privacy.

Chapter 18

Early the next morning, before Dad leaves for work, his phone blasts out a ring. I glance at my own phone and read a blurry six followed by a pair of threes. In the a.m. What kind of legal trouble has someone calling this early?

I stuff my face into my pillow and squeeze my eyes shut, hoping to block the noise. Dad calls to Mom and she grumbles back, unhappy about waking up. Their bedroom door opens and closes. I toss my pillow aside in time to hear the rush of their voices in the hallway. Something big has happened. Something they don't want me to know about.

With a groan, I pull myself out of bed and start dressing for work, using the extra time to plug in my flat iron. When my hair is straightened, I find Mom in the kitchen, mixing up a batch of blueberry muffins. An early morning bake-a-thon is another bad omen. Plus, Dad's car's already gone.

I grab an orange and dig my fingernails into the peel. "Who called?"

"Patti Dalisay." Mom dusts flour off the front of her favorite baking sweatshirt. "Sami's not feeling well. She started running a fever last night."

The air turns liquid. I set down the orange as my appetite dissolves. Heart pounding in my throat, I will myself to calm down. Fevers are common. People get sick. I steady myself by latching on to a chair. "Is she...okay?"

"They took her to the hospital, just to be cautious. After what happened to Emeline, their family doctor wanted to watch Sami. Patti wanted to let Dad know that Braeden won't be at work today." Mom moves around the kitchen, needing to be busy. She opens the dishwasher and unloads the silverware. "Also, last week was Emeline's birthday."

Tiny splinters of sorrow prick my chest. Did Braeden or Sami mention their sister's birthday in passing and I failed to pick up on it? Would I really have missed something so important? Yesterday, at work, Braeden hadn't acted differently. Maybe he assumed Sami told me everything about their sister.

"I want to do something," I say to Mom. "Flowers, maybe? Or I can help you bake something?"

"We should say a prayer for all of them." Mom glances up from her muffin tins. "Go on. I'll be right there."

I head into the living room and click on the LED candles in front of the small statue of Saint Piera. The medal I wear with her likeness weighs heavy on my chest. Rather than recite the familiar lines of my Catholic school prayers, I immediately begin to bargain with God. I may not be the best at praying, but I can wheel and deal like a highly skilled game show host. I offer to trade my own health, my plans to go away to college, even the car Mom and Dad promised to buy me after I get my driver's license. When I run out of words, images of everything I want to exchange in return for Sami's recovery flip through my brain. I hope it's enough to get a message upstairs.

After a few minutes, Mom appears, placing her hand on my shoulder.

"I'll stop by church this morning and talk to Monsignor," she says. "Why don't you try to check in with Braeden later today? I'm sure he needs a friend right now."

Somehow, Mom picked up on the heavy conscience Braeden carries around like a suitcase filled with boulders strapped to his chest.

On my way to work, I pause in front of the Dalisays' house. Further down Chestnut Street, a lawn mower roars to life. Braeden's car sits in the driveway and Mr. Dalisay's daily paper lays in the grass, the plastic cover wet with dew. Mom said they weren't home, but I still knock on the door. No one answers. I pull out my phone and text Braeden.

Heard about Sami. Please let me know how I can help.

When I can't think of another reason to stall outside of their house, I head into town, hoping to use the two-mile hike to the office to find a way to stop my eyes from tearing.

~

No one in the office mentions Braeden by name, but the weight of his absence pushes into my chest. Celeste keeps me busy running documents back and forth to the courthouse. At lunchtime, Mia drops a vanilla milkshake from Summer Creamery on my desk. Even Dad ventures into the file room, asking for an update on my save-the-environment project. Braeden hasn't replied to my text. I send Sami a message, too, but it's not even marked as delivered. The sick feeling in my stomach lingers through the work day and continues as I walk home in the late afternoon heat. When I turn onto our street, I hear a familiar thwack. From two houses away, the rhythm of Braeden's movements appear automatic, like his arm's a robotic hurling machine.

"Hey," I say, stopping at the end of his drive.

Thwack. He catches the ball and flicks his eyes to me. "Hey, Leanne."

I take a cautious step closer. "How's Sami?"

He cocks his arm and lets loose. The ball hits the net and springs right back. *Thwack.* "She's okay. They admitted her for observation, because of our family history." The crack in his voice stabs at my heart. I feel a pull between us, the growing desire to be near him, but he won't even look at me.

"I didn't know it was your sister's birthday," I say. "I'm sorry, Braeden."

"Sami and I didn't want to say anything. She knew your birthday was coming up and...it's a special day for you." After two more throws, he drops out of his stance, the ball clutched tightly in his hand, and taps a code into the pad next to his garage door. The door rolls open and he glances back at me. "I wanted to throw a few before practice. See you later?"

My throat tightens, but I manage to answer. "Of course. Tell Sami I asked about her."

Watching him disappear in the house, my confidence deflates. Should I try harder? Force him to talk to me? I've never felt intolerable before, but Braeden can't even look me in the eye. He threw up a wall between us and I have no idea how to bring it down.

~

"Sami's still in the hospital," I tell Mom when she greets me at the door. The air teems with the aroma of baking chicken, onion and thyme. In the kitchen, a tower of Tupperware sits on the counter. Sometime during the day, Mom graduated from baking muffins to cooking chicken noodle soup, despite the ninety degree temperature. Comfort food knows no season.

"Did you see Patti?" Mom asks, foraging through a drawer and holding up two ladles, one slightly larger than the other. Her collection of utensils could win a prize at the county fair.

"Braeden was outside and I talked to him for a minute." Actually, more like ten seconds.

Mom picks the smaller ladle and skims it through the broth. "I'm sure she's fine. I think the stress of Em's birthday affected all of them. You know how it is."

I do. The weeks before June eighth never fail to throw me off.

"By the way, what do you want to do for *your* birthday this weekend?"

Mom's attempt to cheer me up falls painfully flat. The excitement of turning sixteen is gone. All I can think of is a girl I never met, whose birthday was only days away from mine. She should be here, but she's not.

"The usual, I guess." Traditionally, Mom, Dad, and I take the train into the city. Some years we see a show. When I turned thirteen, Dad suffered through a Taylor Swift concert. It's always been the three of us, sometimes with Callie tagging along, and I never minded—until Braeden. Earlier this summer, I'd thought about celebrating with him, Sami, and Callie, maybe getting all of our families together for a small party. Right now, I know that won't be happening.

"I'll see what's playing downtown," Mom says. "Maybe a show and dinner on the waterfront?"

"Sounds great."

"Dad can take you for your permit test next week. Have you studied?"

"I downloaded the app to take practice tests." I hold up my phone.

"Impressive," she says. "I don't know if I'm ready for you to start driving. What about your birthday cake? Golden pound with raspberry filling?"

"My favorite. Thanks, Mom." I step toward the door. "I need to change before dinner." I tread upstairs and slip out of my work clothes. After throwing on a T-shirt and shorts, I tuck my phone in my pocket, waiting for a call from Braeden that never comes.

~

Braeden's car is missing from his driveway when I leave for work. I start walking toward the office, but my feet feel like they're made of cement. I pause at the corner and a red bus pulls up: the Trolley, which runs a continuous loop around downtown Spring River. The shuttle's ridership mainly consists of senior citizens who can't drive, teens lacking reliable rides, and the occasional energy-conscious commuter. Today, the bus is empty except for one white-haired lady carrying a handful of reusable shopping bags. She gets off in front of the open air farmers' market. I ride to the end of the line, the closest stop to the shrine. From two blocks away, the hammering sounds of the construction crew call to me.

Behind the fence, I pause to note the changes in the tall building since my last visit. The speed of the shrine's transformation leaves me breathless. A white gull perches on the highest peak of the red tile roof, cawing at the bright blue sky. Two men dangle on a scaffold, painting the stucco façade a bright yellow color. The newly-paved walkway intersects two gardens, each with a copper fountain gurgling.

I slip inside, breathing in a smell of fresh sawdust. In the narthex, light filters through the window cut-outs, still waiting for the promised stained glass. The seemingly-untouched marble floor gleams.

In the tower, the nine a.m. Angelus bells toll. I pull out my phone and text Dad, sending him a picture of the shrine-in-process and letting him know I'm on my way to work. For a long time, I gaze through the glass wall, into the silent church, afraid to cross over and invade the holy space. Thoughts of Sami push me forward. I duck into the last pew and begin a quick prayer. The bells continue to ring, covering my whispered words.

Somewhere in the process, tears begin to fall. Out of the corner of my eye, I glimpse someone with blond hair and kind eyes. She says my name in a low voice and I turn to Sister Bernadette.

"Are you enjoying your summer?" she asks.

"I was. But my friend is sick," I whisper, pushing up from the kneeler and resting in the wood pew. "She shouldn't be sick. And her sister—Emeline—I never met her. She died last year. Her family prayed for her and their prayers didn't work."

The accusation pours out of my broken heart. Because I need to understand how this could happen.

Sister sinks down next to me with a sigh. "I'm sorry to hear about your friend and her family, Leanne. I wish I could tell you everything will be okay."

A tidal wave of anger surges within me, halting my tears. "Her name is Sami and she's supposed to start at Holy Family this year. What happened to her sister, Emeline, was unfair. And now Sami is sick, too. Life is so unfair and I don't understand why." I lift my eyes to Sister's, wanting her to see my doubt. "Father Foley, the priest here at the shrine, and Monsignor, too – they want me to stand up and proclaim my holiness. But I can't. They don't understand me at all." The tears start anew. "Sister, I didn't deserve a miracle. So many other people deserve it more than me. And I'm not a perfect person. I'm not even...the most religious person."

Her light eyebrows pop up. "So you don't know why you were chosen?"

I shake my head. "Do you?"

"No, but I believe there was a reason. Although you may need to accept that you'll never know it."

I manage a tight smile. "Sounds easy, right?"

Sister Bernadette shifts beside me, and the pew creaks. "Perhaps. But I think there's a deeper lesson for you to learn. Leanne, your miracle was a gift and I believe on some level, you understand how great a gift it was. You think others are more deserving. But it was not your choice to make." Her eyes float to the front of the church, where the altar is still missing. "Someone thought you needed a miracle."

"Saint Piera," I whisper, clasping the medal around my neck.

"A very holy woman. One of my favorite saints. That's why I'm here today – I couldn't wait to see this place, so I snuck in a little early." Sister makes a sweeping gesture around the church. "Is it everything you expected?"

"I-I'm not sure. I hadn't really set any expectations. I came here today because I wanted to find some way to help my friend and this seemed like the best place to start."

Sister Bernadette nods. "Leanne, I think you're a very bright young girl. You know yourself well and understand who you are...and who you are not. So if you want to help those you care about the most, maybe it's time you discovered your mission."

For the first time I allow myself to glance around the church. I feel the emotions inside me starting to escape, like a slip of air hissing out after the first twist on a bottle cap. I clasp my hands in my lap to keep everything from bubbling over, all at once. "I guess I can try to come up with some way to make the world a better place."

"Of course you can." Sister unleashes a small smile. "So will I see you at the dedication?"

~

For the second day in a row, I walk into work with red eyes.

Celeste gives me a hug. "It's a tough time for all of us. This office is part of my family." I hug her back, breathing in her familiar scent. She sighs. "I've known you since you were a baby, Leanne. I hate to see you so upset."

"It's not me." I pull back. "It's—"

"Braeden. I know. But when you care about someone who's in pain, you hurt, too. And everyone around you hurts." She sighs. "He's not an easy one, is he? But then again, neither are you."

I choke out a laugh right as Braeden blows through the door. Celeste and I watch him push through the waiting area, pausing to pick up a folder with his name on it, muttering something under his breath.

"Good morning to you, too," Celeste says after he disappears into the conference room and shuts the door behind him.

"He's even more upset because last week was—"

"I know." Celeste tugs on the sleeve of her dress. "Mr. Strong told me all about it."

For the next few hours, Braeden buries himself in whatever assignment Dad left for him.

"Why don't you check on him?" Celeste asks after watching me pass by the closed door for the fiftieth time.

"I think he wants to be alone," I say, staring hard at the door, wishing I had x-ray vision. If I knew he was holding up okay in there, I wouldn't be so desperate to talk to him.

Celeste purses her lips. "Did you two have a fight?"

"No." But I sort of wish we had. A loud argument might have cleared the air between us and also given me a clue about why he refuses to even look at me.

She shakes her head and reaches for the ringing phone. "Men. So peculiar."

I avoid the conference room for the rest of the day. He obviously wants a break from me and I'll give it to him...for now.

Around three o'clock, Braeden pops his head into Dad's office, where I'm working at a side table, sifting through a stack of paperwork, marking pages to be scanned.

He places two typed pages on the desk. "I have your summaries."

Dad looks up from his reading and removes his glasses. "Thank you, Braeden. How's Sami?"

Braeden shrugs, looking anywhere but at me. "Better."

"Can I see her?" I ask, emboldened by my father's presence. Surely Braeden won't refuse me in front of his boss.

But Braeden shakes his head, already backing out of the office. "She's still sleeping a lot. I'll tell her to send you a message when she's ready."

After Braeden closes the door, Dad shoots me a sympathetic look. "I'm sure Sami will be fine."

But it's not Sami I'm worried about. It's Braeden.

Chapter 19

Holed up in my bedroom, I push my curtains aside, letting the cooler night air soothe me as I read. The amber spark of headlights rounds the corner and flashes in through the window before Braeden's car turns into his driveway. Over the buzzing of a flickering streetlamp between his house and mine, I hear a door open and close with a muted thud.

My pulse pounds as I shove my feet into my flip-flops. Before I realize it, I'm halfway across the street.

I call his name and he turns to me. Under the silvery moon, heavy circles beneath his eyes look like purple bruises, matching the faded mark on his cheek. I sprint the last ten feet, closing the distance between us and throwing my arms around his waist. His hands press into my back and I realize he's shaking.

"Leanne." His chest heaves as he struggles for a breath. "I knew at some point one of us would get sick, but..."

I bury my face in his shoulder, hiding my fear from him. "Is Sami—?"

"She's fine. Sleeping. Her fever went down." A hollow,

choking sound rises in his throat. "I know this time is different, but going to the hospital brought everything back." He breathes in deeply. "I can't sleep. Do you want to take a ride?"

I pull back. "Right now? Tonight?"

His fingers press my side, like he's afraid I'll run away. "Please. I want to go to the shrine."

I catch the desperation in his eyes. "We can go, but the doors might be locked. I'll call Father Foley." I reach for my phone, in my pocket.

"No." Braeden grabs my hand, gripping my fingers. "Just us. If the doors are locked, we'll leave."

I only hesitate for a heartbeat before sliding into his car. Braeden's hands are still shaking when he grips the steering wheel.

I touch his arm. His skin feels warm. Too warm. "Are you okay to drive?"

"Yeah, I'll be fine." He opens the windows and the moonroof, letting cooler air blow into the car. "Turn on the radio."

I fool around with the stations, but what do you listen to at a time like this? I settle on a station playing instrumental music with heavy keyboards, letting the calming sounds fill the air between us.

At the shrine, Braeden pulls to a stop in front of the gates. An owl hoots her somber greeting as we pass, our steps striking a hurried rhythm over the stone walkway. Braeden grips the heavy handle to open the door and the scent of incense escapes into the night. Inside the dark, silent narthex, smells of new wood, and fresh paint greet us while moonbeams sparkle through open skylights.

"I'm going in," Braeden says, staring into the church. Dozens of LED candles flicker around the altar, which arrived since my last visit.

Braeden advances down the side aisle and lifts a flickering candle from a display. I hear him whisper both his sisters' names. For a long time we stand at the front of the church, the candles forming a curtain of what feels like starlight around us. Tears cling to Braeden's long eyelashes, but he runs his arm over his face to clear them before they fall. After another minute of silence, he reaches for my hand.

"I hate the hospital." His quiet voice breaks the silence. "Sami does too. But, after what happened to Em, we had to take her. She had a fever and couldn't stop coughing. We loaded her in the car and she started crying. Kept saying she didn't want to go back there. Like she thought what would happen to Em might happen to her, too. In the ER, the nurses kept talking to her, trying to calm her until the doctors checked her out."

I squeeze his hand. "I'm sorry you had to go through that again. I know I'm not family, but—"

Braeden waves me off. "It's not that. She counts on you. I count on you...as a friend."

I turn to him, a sinking feeling in my chest. "Is that how you think of me? As a friend?"

If my question surprises him, he doesn't show it. "I don't know," he admits, pressing a hand to his forehead. "I like you a lot, Leanne. But I'm so messed up right now."

His words pierce like a dagger. Taking a deep breath, he continues. "I need to be with my family. Sami and my parents...my head isn't in the right place...it's not fair to you." A shiver rolls through him and his eyes lose their focus. "We should go before someone finds us in here."

I tug on his hand until his eyes return to me. "If you need me...when you need me." I swallow hard. "I'm here."

His head tilts, showing he heard me and understands. After a final glance around the shrine, he drops my hand and walks toward the exit, keeping a step ahead of me. The door hisses as it closes behind us and we step into the warm night.

I can't help wishing Braeden's words could be left behind, trapped in the stony silence of the church, or extinguished as easily as a flicker of candlelight. But again, what's between us has shifted and I'll find a way to deal with the new reality.

On the ride back to Chestnut Street, I struggle to keep my eyes open. The radio plays a long stream of commercials, but neither of us bothers to change the station. For the last mile, I count the dark houses, desperately wanting space between us. The silence from Braeden eats away at me. I wish we could be mad at each other. I want him to tell me he hates me because of what I am. Then I might find a way to accept this new distance between us.

He pulls into my driveway and reaches in the backseat of his car. "This is a birthday present for you, from Sami." He hands me a gift bag.

"When did she get this?"

Braeden runs a hand through his hair. "She's been planning it for a while—ever since she stumbled across your birthday in an old news article. I think she might be your biggest fan. My dad limited our Leanne Strong discussions to no more than thirty minutes per day in our house."

"I-I can't take it," I say, pushing the bag back in his hand.

"It's a gift. Sami wants you to have it." Braeden offers me a sad smile. "Don't make me go back to the hospital and tell her I didn't give it to you." He pries open my clenched fingers and places the handle of the bag in my palm.

I open the door and run from the car before he sees my tears.

Chapter 20

After a sleepless night, morning light breaks through my curtains as I open Sami's present. Inside the gift bag, wrapped in tissue paper, I find a scrapbook. On the first page, she taped a recent picture of the shrine in progress. I flip through more photos and news clippings arranged by date, beginning with the first magazine article describing my miracle.

Sami recorded my story, as seen through her eyes. For the first time, I'm on the outside looking in, watching my life unfold from a new perspective. The awe in my mother's face in a picture of her watching me walk. My father's smile when the announcement is made that my miracle was confirmed.

The final page, dated yesterday, shows the shrine at twilight, with the sun falling behind the Spanish-tiled roof. Braeden must have snapped the photo for his sister.

I'm still flipping pages when Callie calls.

"Happy birthday, friend," she says. "What did your boy get you?"

"He's not mine. Not anymore." I fill her in on my latest trip to the shrine.

"He's conflicted," Callie decides. "But I wouldn't give up on him. I'm sure he still wants to be with you."

I lean into the heap of pillows stacked against my headboard, cradling my phone against my ear. "And what am I supposed to do with that?"

"Give him space. Date someone else while he sorts everything out."

"Come on, Callie. He's the only person I've ever wanted to seriously date. I'm not exactly someone who jumps between boyfriends."

"Not yet, but now that you've been with one good-looking guy you'll probably want to make it a habit."

"It's not like that. And I'm not interested in anyone else."

"Why not? You didn't fall in love, did you?" The bitterness in Callie's voice practically singes my eardrum.

"No. But he was worth breaking my no-dating rule. I can't think of anyone else who might change my mind."

"Not Jake?"

"Definitely not Jake."

"I'll think of someone for you. Until then, let's do a best friends thing to celebrate your birthday. Want to drown your sorrows in ice cream?"

"Ice cream and tennis. I haven't been to the club at all this summer."

Callie huffs through the phone. "Fine. I'll let you beat me in tennis, but only because it's your special day. Be ready in an hour."

I page through the book once more before dropping it back in the gift bag and sending Sami a message saying thank you for the birthday gift, adding best wishes for her speedy recovery.

When Callie pulls in our driveway, I notice an unfamiliar

car in front of the Dalisays'. Their front door swings open and ex-neighbor Harper walks out with Braeden. I duck into Callie's car before he catches me spying.

Callie notices the couple as we cruise toward his house. "Who's the girl with Braeden?"

"His old neighbor. And she's also an ex-girlfriend. Sami really likes her." But Sami likes me too. She made me a scrapbook. I wonder if she ever put a scrapbook together for Harper. Then I feel horrible for thinking that way.

"He's hanging out with his ex? That stinks rottenly." Callie glares at Braeden, not that he sees her. He's solely focused on Harper as she talks and flails her arms. "She looks kind of...mad."

"Who knows?" I ask, not in the mood to dwell on Harper's current mood.

"Want me to pull over?"

"No, I want you to drive faster. I'll hide."

Callie stomps on the gas and I duck my head. When we're past the Dalisays', I glance in the rear view mirror. Harper's face is pressed into Braeden's chest and her shoulders are heaving. I gnaw on my bottom lip, worried about Sami. Braeden would tell me if she took a turn for the worse. No matter what happens between him and Harper, he knows I care about his sister.

Still, the sight of Braeden with another girl in his arms shreds my heart into tiny, lovesick pieces.

~

After my birthday dinner and a movie in town with my parents, I plan on finishing the night by crawling into bed with a book. I haven't shown Mom or Dad the gift from Sami. It feels like a secret between me and her and I'm reluctant to share it, even with my parents. I page through the scrapbook again, soft lamplight spilling on the pages, taking in the history of my miracle. Seeing all the other people involved in the process has me questioning my choices. Have I been selfish? When I was younger and didn't understand why people were so interested in me, I made a decision to protect myself, one my parents have always supported. Now, I'm older and the walls I built as a small child are starting to press in on me.

I check my phone for messages from Braeden or Sami and try to push aside my hurt over the empty text stream.

Hoping for a distraction, I call Callie. I need to hear her familiar chatter about Gavin or listen to her threaten to drag me to another terrible movie on our summer watch list. But even she's busy tonight. When the call goes to voicemail, I send her a text.

Call me, Callie. I need to talk to you.

Her response doesn't come. Instead, the house phone rings. Mom's light steps pause outside of my bedroom and she calls my name, making sure I'm awake. She taps open my door and hands me the phone. "Callie's mother wants to talk to you."

"Leanne, have you talked to Callie?" Mrs. Perkins asks.

"I called and texted her today, but she hasn't called back."

"She's missing. She ran out of the house this afternoon and her phone battery must have died."

Icy fear slithers through my veins. "She's been gone all day?"

"I'm calling the police if I don't find her soon," Mrs. Perkins is saying. "If you hear from her, tell her she needs to come home."

I text Callie again, hoping she thought to bring a charger with her. After four more messages and two phone calls, I start to make a list of where she could be. I text all the Girlfriends, but no one's seen her all day. I pace the room, wondering what to do next, digging my fingernails into my skin, leaving a trail of half-moon marks on my arm.

"Is everything all right?" Mom asks, knocking on my door again.

Callie's impulsive, but she's not careless enough to drink and drive or break a law.

I answer through the door, deciding not to worry my mother just yet. "Callie's not feeling well. I called her a bunch of times to tell her about my birthday dinner. Mrs. Perkins wanted me to know Callie's.... unavailable." The lie pokes a hole in my chest, but I force words out.

I wrap a blanket around me and lower myself onto the bed, my knees knocking together despite the warm air in my room. When I can't stare at my silent phone for another minute, I glance out the window. Yellow light shines behind the blinds on the second floor of the Dalisay's house. I jump from the bed, shove my feet into flip flops and race down the stairs. "Braeden's home. I want to see if he has news about Sami."

Mom pokes her head out of the kitchen. "This late? I don't know, Leanne. Is Patti home too?" She cranes her neck to check our neighbor's driveway.

"I'll stay outside if you're worried."

"It's not that I don't trust him—"

"I understand. I won't be long." I'm out the door before she can ask another question.

I ring the Dalisays' doorbell three times.

"Leanne?" Braeden answers, wearing a pair of mesh basketball shorts, his hair damp from the shower. I try very hard to ignore his bare chest.

"Callie's missing. I need to talk to Jake's friend, Gavin. Do you know how to get in touch with either of them?"

Braeden runs a hand through his hair, leaving a row of spiky tufts in his wake. "I think Jake lives in one of those big homes out by the lake."

"North of town?"

"Yeah. One of the guys on the team pointed out his house when we drove by. Jake's dad's some big architect and they live in a mansion – like an old stone castle, but with solar panels on the roof. I think I'd remember it." Braeden retreats into his house. I wait on their front porch until he returns, pulling a gray T-shirt over his head.

"Let's take a ride," he says.

I text Mom and tell her Braeden and I are going for a late-night ice cream run, like any innocent pair of teenagers, and shove my phone back in my pocket before she responds.

"You don't have to do this," I start to protest. "You hardly know Callie. I'm sure I can find Jake's house if you give me the description again."

"You're not going to that guy's house alone," Braeden says. "And how do you plan on getting there—on your bike?"

"But Sami—"

"My parents are with Sami. They practically threw me out of the hospital. Told me to go home and rest."

"Then you need to sleep."

"I'm not tired." Eyebrows slanted together, he stalks past me, into his car, waiting for me to follow.

We drive five miles north and veer onto a slice of road wrapping around the lake, running in front of a row of huge estates overlooking the dark water. Braeden stops in front of a massive stone structure complete with turrets and Gothic arches. Church-like, but without crosses or a steeple. I can see why Mr. Maddaloni was asked to design the shrine.

Without waiting for me, Braeden storms up to the entryway and pounds on the door. On the other side, loud music cuts off and someone yells for everyone to quiet down. After a brief silence, Jake cracks open the door.

His eyes narrow when he recognizes Braeden. "Looking for a fight, Dalisay?"

Braeden folds his arms over his chest. "I'm looking for Callie Perkins. Is she here?"

Jake shrugs. "There's a lot of people here."

A muscle in Braeden's jaw twitches. "Go get your friend Gavin."

Jake raises his hand to slam the door shut.

I step around Braeden. "Please, Jake. Callie's missing and her mom's ready to call the police."

Scowling, Jake drops his hand and stalks away, leaving the door open. Braeden wraps his hand around my elbow and we skirt around a group of guys huddled in the hallway. Jake heads toward an open staircase, descending into the basement, where we find Gavin alone, on a leather sofa, watching baseball on a muted television.

"Dude, where's Callie? Wasn't she here earlier?" Jake asks his friend.

Gavin points the remote control in his hand toward a blanket-covered lump on the floor with a lock of blond hair poking out. "She fell asleep. She was upset and I told her to stay here with me."

I shake Callie. "Wake up. Your mom's looking for you."

Callie's eyelids flutter. "Leanne? What time is it?"

Braeden helps me boost her to a sitting position. Streaks of mascara fan out from her eyes, evidence of her tears. I hug her gently. "I'm here. I'll take you home."

She brushes her fingers over my cheek, like she's not sure

if I'm real. "You're glowing."

"What?" I turn to Braeden and he shrugs. Behind me, a pendant light dangles from the ceiling. Maybe it's hitting me at an odd angle. "Listen to me, Callie. Your mom wants to call the police."

"Let her call," Callie grumbles, more alert now. "I'm not going home. My parents can yell and scream at each other all they want. But I'm done."

"Come to my house, then. You can't stay here all night."

Groaning, Callie pushes to her feet. "Where's Gavin?"

I check the sofa he'd crashed on, but he's disappeared. "Around here somewhere. Jake knows we're taking you home."

Callie glances over her shoulder once more as we climb the stairs, but Gavin has deserted her. When we get to the dark first floor I'm completely lost. Braeden strides ahead, eventually finding the front door and pushing outside without a word to anyone.

I pile a trembling Callie into the back seat.

"Is she sick?" Braeden asks, cracking the window. "I'll pull over."

"I'm okay. Just upset," Callie says in a weak voice. "I'm in so much trouble for running away. I don't want to go home." She lifts her teary eyes to mine. "But I'm so tired, Leanne. So tired of dealing with their constant crap."

"Why didn't you call me?" I ask, touching her arm. "I would have helped you."

Callie turns to look out the window. "Gavin was on the phone when the fighting started. He heard my mom screaming. He offered to pick me up. I just...needed to get away. So I told him to meet me at the end of the street. I packed a bag—oh shoot, I lost my bag."

"We'll find it. I can go back to Jake's—"

"I'll call him," Braeden cuts in from the front seat. "I'll get his number."

I imagine Braeden is white-knuckling the steering wheel at the thought of knocking on Jake's door again.

"I'll text Gavin," Callie insists and pulls her phone from her pocket. At least she was smart enough to keep her cell with her. "Shoot. My battery died."

"What's his number?" I ask, pulling out my phone.

"I don't have it memorized. I forgot my charger." She grips my arm. "Gavin cares about me. That's why I left."

"I care about you too. Callie. You can always call me. You know that, right?"

Nodding, she leans back and closes her eyes, mumbling something about not ruining my birthday weekend. I pull out my own phone, deciding to clue my parents in on the situation before I bring Callie home. "I'll have my mom call your mom. We can tell her that you're staying with us tonight and you'll be home tomorrow."

"Thanks, Leanne," Callie whispers, reaching out and squeezing my arm. "And Braeden. Thank you, too."

At my house, she ducks out of the car and takes a seat on the porch step to wait for me.

Braeden steps out of the car and we face each other, the heavy night air swarming around us.

"I'm sorry for bothering you tonight. When I saw the light in your house, I was worried about Callie and I didn't stop to think. I just...needed help," I stammer. My heart races from the nervous excitement of being close enough to feel the warmth rolling off his skin. The memory of our kisses ignites a longing that pulls through my entire body.

"You had a good reason," he says. "Besides, I owe you for

everything you've done for Sami."

I dart my eyes to Callie to make sure she's okay. She's sitting on an wicker chair, star-gazing.

Chin lifted, I turn back to Braeden. "I won't claim to understand everything going on with you right now," I say, working hard to maintain a physical distance from him. "But I can tell when you're upset."

"I know you want to help," he says, his voice tired and hoarse. "But sometimes I think of Emeline...the night she died." His voice breaks, along with my heart. "Leanne...it's just that...I still can't accept what happened to her. It makes no sense. She was a good person, too."

I swallow hard, my throat dry and tight. "I'm sorry. I'm so, so sorry."

I can't be here, looking at him right now. He's telling me his truth, pouring out the raw pain inside of him. It probably hurts him just to look at me. Because it makes no sense that I experienced the one thing he wanted for his sister.

I force my body to turn away, to leave him at the end of the driveway and join Callie on the porch. Together, we watch Braeden back his car down the street, into his driveway.

"That is one majorly conflicted boy," she says, shaking her head.

Now it's my turn to cry.

Callie wraps an arm around my shoulders. "You know what? I think he wants to be with you, Leanne, but he doesn't know how to make it work. I couldn't help watching you and honestly, I've never seen two people try harder to stay away from each other. I have no idea what you were talking about, but it was awful to watch."

I wipe a tear from my cheek. "I made a mistake. I should have stuck to my non-dating plan. Then neither of us would be hurting."

I wait for her to agree, but instead she says, "I'm proud of you because you took a risk. You needed to do it, for yourself and for Braeden, too."

"I don't know anymore." I wait for my breathing to slow down and the ache in my chest to ease. "Did you call your mom?"

She passes my phone back. "Dad's gone. He decided to move out for a few weeks and give everyone some space. Mom wants me to come home."

"Of course she does."

Callie sighs. "I don't hate them. I just hate living with them."

"Things will get better, right? Your dad will find a job. They'll work everything out and he'll be back."

"Maybe yes, maybe no. Sometimes relationships are just broken. And nothing you can do will fix them."

She's talking about her parents, I tell myself. But in my heart, I suspect she's also trying to warn me about hoping for anything more from Braeden.

Chapter 21

Walking to work, my heart hammers in my chest. Another day of sharing office space with Braeden is almost too much to bear. My head hurts at the thought of forcing myself to focus on work while pretending to ignore him.

Celeste hands me a cup of tea, like she knows the morning has already slid downhill. She must have seen Braeden. I take my drink into the file room. When I flip on the light, Braeden appears and I jump.

He rubs his red eyes. "I couldn't find the switch."

I set my tea on a table before I drop it, and take a deep breath. "How's Sami?"

He pulls a file from the shelf and heads for the exit. "She's coming home today. How's Callie?"

"Home, too. Her dad left for a while." Before he disappears, I ask, "Can I see her? Sami?"

His eyes catch mine in a fleeting glance. "Text her. She has her phone." With that, he hurries off.

~

I don't see Braeden again until the end of the day, when he rushes out the door, almost taking me down in the hallway. He pauses, hands curled into fists at his sides. "Sami asked about you. Twice. Do you have time—"

"I can leave now."

"Ride with me, then."

A hundred questions swirl in my head on the way back to Chestnut Street, but I can't work up the courage to ask them. Braeden turns the radio on and the music covers our silence.

Mr. Dalisay is home, pacing around the house like he's not sure what to do with himself. When he sees me, the worried set of his jaw eases. "Nice to see you. Sami's in her room, getting settled."

Braeden calls his sister. "Someone's here to see you."

"Leanne?" Sami's voice is weak.

Mrs. Dalisay pokes her head into the hallway. "Come on in, Leanne."

I flash Braeden a look and he seems to recognize my fear.

"Talk to her," he says. "She'll tell you what she needs."

The walls in Sami's bedroom are light pink and the furniture is all white. Sami lifts her head off the stack of pillows, pushing herself up on the bed when she sees me. A bone at the base of her wrist bumps out when she reaches for a glass of water on the bedside table.

"Hey, Sami," I whisper. "Are you feeling better?"

"Yes," she says, though her lower lip trembles. "I wasn't as sick as Em."

I lower myself onto the mattress, folding my hands in my lap. "Do you want to talk about it?"

She sinks back into the pillows and shifts her gaze to the window. "I thought I was fine, just a little cough, but it kept getting worse. At the hospital, I was really scared. And I started to think about Em, when she was there. How the doctors and nurses tried so hard to help her...but they couldn't."

I smooth out a wrinkle in the quilt covering her bed. "Did someone help you? Like, a doctor or nurse?"

"Yes, they talked to me." Turning to face me, she dips her chin. "We moved and it's been over a year since Emeline died. I didn't think I'd ever feel that sad again. But I did and it really hurt."

I hesitate, unsure what to say next. I decide to keep asking questions, and let her choose how to answer. "Do you want to talk to me about her? Now?"

She reaches for a small fabric-covered book, on the table. "Will you look at the memory book I made for her? Because it's hard for me to...just talk about her. But I want you to know who she was."

"I'd like that." I take the journal and turn it back and forth in my hands. "And I want to thank you for my birthday present. No one's ever given me a gift like that. I haven't shown it to my parents yet, because I wanted to talk to you first."

A cough rattles in her chest. She takes a slow breath and another sip of water. "I missed Em so much and when we moved here...and you were so nice. When I found out about your miracle, it made me think...that not everything is sad. You gave me hope."

I move closer to Sami and squeeze her hand. "You're allowed to be sad sometimes. I don't think it's possible to always be happy. But when you're really sad and you need to talk about it, I'm here for you. Always."

Sami watches me flip through the pages of her book. When I pause at a picture of her with Emeline and her brother, she says, "You should talk to Braeden. He was really upset when I got sick."

I glance up from the page. The hope shining in her eyes is hard to ignore. "Yeah, he's kind of...tough."

Sami starts to laugh. "He's a huge pain in the neck, you mean."

I give her a half-smile. "He has reasons." A thought strikes me, and before I think too hard about it, I unclasp my Saint Piera medal. "This is for you," I say as I gently fasten the medal around Sami's neck. "Wear it until you feel better."

She holds the medal between her thumb and forefinger, fighting back tears. "Thank you, Leanne."

A doorbell chimes below us. Reluctant to leave, I close the book and hand it back to her. "You have another visitor. I should go."

From the second floor, I catch a glimpse of Harper and Braeden near the front of the house.

"I don't understand why I can't see her," she says.

"Only family members," Braeden replies, standing guard in the foyer. "She's still sick. She's not supposed to be around a lot of people right now. Her immune system needs time to build up again."

At this point, Harper looks up and notices me, hovering at the top of the stairs. "She's not family, is she?" If she could fire arrows from her fingertips, I suspect I'd be her main target.

The air thickens as we wait for Braeden's answer. He casts a glance over his shoulder and waves me into the foyer. "Leanne, thanks for stopping by. I'll catch up with you later."

Head held high, I squeeze between them and march out the front door. By the time I reach my house and check Braeden's driveway, Harper's car is gone.

Chapter 22

Mr. Dalisay calls Dad and asks if Braeden can take a few weeks off from work, but he doesn't give a specific reason for the absence. Of course Dad says yes.

Once they hear the news, Mia and Celeste act as if Braeden never existed. We carry on, working as if it's any other summer, before the Dalisays moved to town. Before the shrine cast a shadow over my life. Although I dreaded the idea of working with Braeden and not speaking to him, the thought of not seeing him every day is a thousand times worse. At least when he was here, in the office, I knew he was okay. Now I wonder if he's not okay...and I wonder if I should be doing *something* to help him.

Over the next few days, I send Sami a message or two, checking in, and she responds with a brief reply. She doesn't mention her brother and I refuse to ask pointed questions just for the sake of pulling information from her. If Braeden and I are never together again, I suppose I'll learn to deal with it. But right now, stuck in the in-between, life is pure torture. I constantly remind myself that he pushed me away. He needs to take the first step back. Until then, I'll find a way to move forward, alone.

Friday night, I'm awake past midnight, thinking of the pictures in Sami's memory book. Sami and Emeline in pigtails at dance recitals. Braeden holding Emeline on his shoulders, watching a parade. The three of them at a baseball game. Smiling. Always smiling together.

I lay on my side, facing the window that gives me a direct view of Braeden's bedroom. His yellow light flicks on. I blink, thinking I must be dreaming. A shadow moves behind the blinds, prompting me to sit up and rub my eyes. I watch the back and forth movement. He's pacing. I can practically feel his anxiety from across the street. The overwhelming sense of needing to be with him rushes through me. I clutch the blanket high over my chest. I miss him so much it hurts to breathe.

My body trembles under the restraint of forcing myself to stay in bed. Eventually, I drift to sleep facing Braeden's window. Hours later, I wake to bright sunlight and my phone chiming in a message from Callie.

Callie: *Go for a run?*

Me: *Yes. Ten minutes. My place.*

I secure my hair in a tight ponytail and dig in my closet for my running shoes. By the time I leave the house, Callie is on my driveway, jogging in place. Field hockey practices start in two weeks, and until then she needs a training partner. As we run, she talks about work. To escape the drama with her parents, she's thrown her energy into the camp job and surprised herself by realizing how much she loves working with kids. While I'm breathless from keeping her pace, she repeats all the funny things they say to her.

"And you wouldn't believe how many parents I've called because they're late picking up their kids." She huffs. "I mean, who forgets their own child?"

I mutter my agreement, if only to keep Callie happy. "Maybe they're stuck in traffic or something."

"Yeah, something. Anyway, I'm the best arts and crafts counselor ever. The fifth graders tell me I'm epic," she says.

"Are you bribing them with candy?" I squeeze out the words between gulps of oven-temperature air.

She smiles, knowing she's busted, and tosses her blond ponytail over her shoulders. "Laffy Taffy is magical."

After we're finished, we cool down by walking up and down the block, which also gives me an excuse to look for Braeden.

"How's your mom?"

"Eh. She'll be okay. Dad's back and they're actually getting along, for once. Maybe they missed each other."

"Good to hear. And how's Gavin?"

Callie snorts. "Him? We're over. He was fun for the summer, but when school starts, we'll never see each other."

"Great," I say.

She digs her elbow into my side. "Yeah, it is great. I'm free to pursue other guys. So, is Braeden back on the market?"

I trip over a crack in the sidewalk and go down hard.

Callie yelps. "Sorry, Leanne! I'm kidding. Braeden is yours, and even if you never get back together, I wouldn't go after him. You know that, right?" She plops down next to me and starts to laugh.

"Sure you wouldn't. Ouch. It hurts," I whine, wiping the sweat tricking down my face with the back of my also-sweaty forearm. I'm a ball of perspiration.

She grabs my scratched up knee between her hands to examine the injury. "Want to run cold water over it? Do you need a band-aid? Or a lollipop?"

I throw her a sideways glance. "Do you have any of those things with you?"

"No. But that's how I distract the camp kids when they're in pain."

I'd gladly let someone dump a bucket of ice water on my head if it would numb the ache in my heart.

~

Another week and no sign of Braeden. Sami hasn't texted much either, except to keep me up to date on the novel she's reading.

Friday morning, Dad strides into the file room, looking for me. "Let's have a talk. In my office."

We pass the front desk, where Celeste's nails cease to hunt and peck on her keyboard. "Uh-oh. Somebody's in trouble."

I drop my stack of papers in her in-box and sigh. "Can you fire your own family?"

Dad glances over his shoulder. "You're not fired, Leanne. Not yet, anyway."

When we're situated in seats around the conference table, I set my shoulders and prepare for the worst. "What do you need me to do?"

Leaning back in his chair, Dad crosses his arms over the front of his suit jacket. "Actually, I thought you might need me. Do you want me to look over your speech?"

My heart starts to pound. "What speech?"

"The speech you're working on for tomorrow's shrine dedication. You are going to say something, aren't you?"

I shift uncomfortably. "Father Foley said I just needed to be there. Not talk."

Dad levels a serious gaze my way. "Leanne, Father Foley may be happy to have you just sit there and smile, but I sense that he's a big pushover." Standing, he removes his jacket and drapes it over the back of the chair. Then, he collapses back into the chair and reaches for a legal pad laying in the center of the table before removing a pen from the pocket on the front of his button-down shirt. "I think you should say something. People are traveling thousands of miles to see you."

"Not me," I insist, gripping the arms of the chair until my fingers are numb. "They're coming for the shrine."

Dad arches an eyebrow. "But you're the primary reason for the shrine's existence in Spring River."

I lean my elbows on the table and sink my chin into my hands. For a while Dad and I stare each other down. From the first second I heard about the shrine, I knew that eventually I'd need to explain my hesitation about making an appearance at the dedication.

"It's not that I don't want to be there," I say. "But I really can't. I'm not the right person to talk to other people about faith and miracles. I'm not a theological scholar. I haven't dedicated my life to religion. I'm only sixteen, for goodness sake. What if I say the wrong thing?"

"If God wanted a religious scholar up on that podium tomorrow, he would have healed a scholar. He wants you, Leanne." Dad pauses and rubs his temples. "Think of Mom. She'll never try to push you to stand in front of a crowd and speak, but deep down, she really wants this." He taps his pen on his desk. "Plus, if I listen to someone who wasn't actually in your bedroom on June eighth tell me about your miracle one more time, I might decide to make up my own story about that night."

He drums his hands on the tabletop, waiting me out. Dad has the patience of an arctic explorer trying to measure the speed of a glacier. When I lift my eyes to his, he seems to know he's won. "You have the ability to inspire people in a different way than the scholars. I promise you, nothing you say will be wrong. As your assistant speechwriter, I guarantee it."

I wriggle under his steady gaze. "You know how much I hate talking in public."

"I do," Dad agrees, but he refuses to let me off the hook. Instead, he leans back in his chair, anticipating my next argument. Classic lawyer move.

As we lapse into a stalemate, I wait for some kind of sign from heaven to tell me what to do. But the only picture in my head is Sami's scrapbook version of my miracle. She said I showed her that life doesn't always have to be sad. If she were sitting here with me now, I know what she'd tell me to do.

I press up from my seat, and pick a pen out of the fancy marble container sitting on Dad's desk. "Pass over one of your legal pads. I'll write my own first draft."

Chapter 23

Mom and I shopped for new dresses for the dedication; mine is yellow and hers is a floral green and pink. My hair is brushed straight, with the front layer braided and swept to the side. Dad wears a new suit with a yellow tie Mom picked out for him. When we pull up in front of the shrine, the construction fence is gone and the façade sparkles under the bright sun.

We pass a quartet of the Sisters of Saint Piera dressed in gray, chattering in a Sicilian dialect as they meander through the gardens where the twin copper fountains gurgle and late-summer wildflowers bloom in a rainbow of colors.

Dad reaches first for Mom's hand and then mine. The three of us face the line of reporters blocking the atrium entrance. Ignoring my weak knees, I struggle to work up a smile for the cameras aimed at my face.

"Will you be speaking during mass, Miss Strong?" someone asks.

"Y-Yes." I manage one shaky word before Dad tugs on my hand and guides me inside. Light pours through the stained glass windows, bathing the marble floors with a kaleidoscope of reds, purples and yellows. In the narthex, glittery mosaics depict the life of Saint Piera, including her first miracle, the curing of a blind woman, half a world away. The super-sized mural of my miracle takes up an entire wall.

"It's beautiful," Mom says, unable to take her eyes off of baby me.

"You should be in the picture," I tell her, realizing for the first time something isn't quite right.

"No, I don't want to be in it," she says, still staring.

"If I'm in it, you should be too." I point to a small corner section of the wall, left clean. "There's room to add a picture of you praying. After all, asking for help was your idea."

She smiles. "The response was something beyond my wildest dreams."

I slide my arms around her. "Thank you, Mom. I'll never be able to say it enough."

She holds me close. "I know you're grateful, Leanne. You don't need to tell me." She sweeps her gaze over the long mural. "The morning I found you—standing, reaching for me—I knew you understood what had happened. It was amazing to see the smile on your face and how proud you were, standing in the crib, waiting for me to find you."

"Good job, Amelia. Now we're all crying," Dad says, his eyes misty.

"Ah, Leanne's here," Father Foley says, breezing over and interrupting our sweet moment before I sob through my makeup. "Welcome, Mr. and Mrs. Strong."

Father Foley leads us on a quick tour around the church, pausing here and there to flip up a kneeler or brush an invisible speck of dust from a pew. An organist arrives and begins practicing while altar servers check the hundreds of candles, making sure they're all lit properly. By the time we return to the narthex, the first visitors have begun to filter inside. Old and young, some wearing Saint Piera medals like the one I gave to Sami. Some recognize me and I do my best to welcome those who greet me by name. Everyone passing by seems to smile at me. I smile back, at least until my face hurts.

"Leanne has prepared a short speech for today," Dad says to Father Foley. "If you'd still like her to address the crowd."

Father looks at me and grins widely, like he knew I'd come around. "Of course. We'd be honored to hear from your daughter."

Waiting for the dedication to start, I sit between my parents in the front row, my knee bouncing up and down. As we settle into the pew and review the order of events, Father tells us he allowed only one video camera inside the church. "This is a holy service, not a Broadway show."

By the time trumpets blare and the long procession of priests, deacons, and bishops begins, every seat is filled. The overflow crowd stands in the narthex, spilling outside, watching the festivities on giant screens.

A long drum roll is followed by the tapping of snares. Bells ring from the high tower and the organ begins to sing. The bishop appears, wearing a tall hat and red robes decorated with gold piping.

For most of the ceremony my mind is focused on the speech crumpled in my sweaty hands. I breathe in and out through my nose, hoping to keep my heart from leaping out of my ribcage. But my nerves get the best of me and I miss my first call to the altar. Dad nudges me with his elbow and Mom squeezes my hand.

My heels click on the marble as I approach the podium and the crowd falls silent.

A wisp of static coughs out of the microphone when I tilt

it down to my level. My hands shake, blurring the words on the paper in front of me. Thankfully, I memorized the speech after practicing in front of my parents for hours last night.

"Um, hello. Good morning. My name is Leanne Strong." My name echoes through the microphone, bouncing off the walls of the church. A few people return my greeting. "Today, I'd like to share the story of my miracle. I was born with a spinal cord defect. Although I don't remember how it felt, my parents have described the daily challenges I faced. These were predicted to be life-long challenges, unless doctors could correct my spine with extensive surgeries. But, shortly before my first birthday, my mother received a relic from a priest who'd recently traveled to Rome. The relic was a piece of fabric taken from the robe of Saint Piera." I lift my eyes from my paper and search for Mom. When I find her in the crowd, she smiles. "The morning after my mother prayed to Saint Piera, I stood on my own for the first time. Soon, I was walking. Developmentally, I caught up to other kids my age within a matter of weeks."

A murmur rolls through the pews, sounds of surprise even though most people in attendance must know my story.

When the crowd quiets, I continue. "I still don't understand why I was chosen for this miracle. I don't feel as if I'm special. So many others in this world face greater challenges than I did." I pause and think of Sami, Braeden and their parents. The light from the chandeliers hanging above me seems to grow fuzzy. I grip the sides of the podium and steady myself before reading my final paragraph.

"Since I was young enough to talk about what happened, people have asked me to describe the miracle. But I never felt as if I could properly put the experience into words. I am not an expert on miracles. I'm not an expert in faith. I still find it hard to define what happened to me. But, if you asked me for the truth...for my truth?" I lift my eyes to the congregation. "I am here today to tell you that miracles happen. And to let you know that I believe I was cured through the power of faith and love. I want all of you to know that I will pray for you every day. If I could give part of myself to help each of you the way I've been helped, I would."

Just then, the doors in the back glide open. I blink into the stream of light pouring through the glass walls separating the narthex and the church. The Dalisay family materializes at the very back of the crowd. Braeden, in a navy blue suit and tie. Sami, walking next to him, a yellow sequined headband decorating her long dark hair. She's thin and pale, but smiling.

I switch my attention back to Braeden, and despite the distance of an entire church between us, I spot the warmth in his eyes. Sami raises her hand to her chest, and holds up my Saint Piera medal. The gold disc catches a ray of sunshine and sparks seem to fly over the high, white walls. I blink into the brightness and the scene in front of me slowly shifts back into place. Most people in the church are still focused on me. The lone cameraman creeps closer, aiming for a tighter shot, reminding me exactly how many eyes are watching my every move.

Father Foley shuffles the papers on his lap when he shifts in his chair, nodding at me to continue. Oh, right. I'm supposed to be giving a speech. I take a deep breath, and carry on. "I hope to inspire all of you by living a life deserving of my miracle. I'm not perfect, but I will try to find my mission and be what God wants me to be. Thank you, Saint Piera. Thank you, Mom and Dad. And thank you to Father Foley, who's overseen the building of this beautiful shrine. May all those who visit this place be blessed with peace and love."

The crowd begins to applaud. I step down from the podium and into the center aisle.

In the back of the church, Braeden raises his hands, clapping along with everyone else. He takes one step forward and smiles, as if to say he's proud of me.

Chapter 24

As soon as the parade of bishops and priests march back down the aisle, the church begins to clear out. Sami presses through the crowd, her yellow headband moving in the opposite direction of the mass exodus, meeting me in the middle of the church.

"You're okay?" I ask her.

She breaks out in a wide grin. "Much better. When I heard you were giving a speech, I told my parents we had to be here."

I cast a glance in my parents' direction, eyes narrowed. "I just decided to give the speech yesterday. Who spilled my secret?"

Sami tilts her head toward our mothers, standing together and admiring the church. "The Chestnut Street gossip committee might have dropped a few hints."

As Dad and Mr. Dalisay stand off to the side talking, I look for Braeden, who's managed to fade into the background.

"Where's your brother—" I start to ask.

"Leanne, I want to show you something." Dad interrupts

me before Sami answers my question. The Dalisays follow my parents and me to a small alcove on the side of the church, close to where Braeden and I stood when we came here alone, together. A marble statue of a young girl holding flowers is surrounded by tables of new, unlit candles.

"Since the announcement of the shrine, there's been a jump in donations coming in through your website," Dad says. "I spoke with Father Foley and we decided to contribute something in memory of Emeline. A candle garden of sorts."

I lean over the rail and touch the foot of the statue. "If I could have asked for anything, this would have been it. I love it, Dad."

A hand touches my shoulder. "If Em was here today, she'd love it, too," Braeden says.

~

Outside, the Bishop bestows a final blessing on the new shrine and the media descends upon us. Photographers jockey for the best position to snap pictures of the miracle girl. I smile and hold my shoulders straight, doing my best to appear appreciative of the attention. I'm happy because Sami's happy. Braeden's happy. Our parents are beyond happy. At this minute, I don't care if the whole world knows what baby Leanne Strong looks like at the age of sixteen.

When the crowds thins and the reporters flock toward Father Foley and the bishop for a more detailed Q&A session, I lead Braeden and Sami over to a group of teachers from Holy Family High, gathered in the back of the narthex.

"Well, Miss Strong, are you happy with the finished product?" asks Sister Bernadette. Colored light from the stained glass dances in her faded blue eyes.

"Yes, I am. Today, this is the most beautiful place in the

world."

She nods. "A step above our school chapel. And large enough to hold graduation ceremonies. Who are your friends?" She turns to Braeden and Sami. "New recruits for my library?"

"Definitely one new recruit." I tug Sami closer, knocking her slightly off balance. "I might have mentioned her to you the last time we spoke. Sami has already read every book included in the language arts curriculum. Most of them twice."

Sami's cheeks turn pink.

Sister Bernadette looks impressed. "I'll have a few new additions this year. I hope you haven't read all of those."

"Actually, I haven't read much lately," Sami admits.

"And, Sister, I know you like baseball," I say, remembering the Red Sox banners posted on the wall in her office. "Braeden could take Holy Family to the state championship."

Sister makes a clucking sound behind her teeth. "It would be nice to have a winning team for a change. Can you promise me a title, young man?"

At this remark Braeden has the good grace to look embarrassed. I shoot him an innocent smile. After everything I've survived this morning, talking in front of thousands of people and being interviewed multiple times for television stations around the world, he deserves some attention, too.

"I'll do my best," he says.

Mr. Dalisay and my dad appear on the far side of the atrium, waving us over.

"Father Foley showed us a secret back exit," Dad says, tilting his head toward a small door that may or may not be a confessional. "The media's wrapping up their coverage. We should sneak out of here before they ask for more footage."

"Do you think the reporters will camp out in front of our

house?" I ask Mom when we find her and Mrs. Dalisay studying a painting of a young Saint Piera.

Mom drags her eyes from the artwork. She might never leave this place. "I think we're safe. The shrine's opening is the big news of the day. And I would guess that next June eighth, everyone will pray here, rather than our front yard. Do you agree, Jason?"

"It's much nicer to sit in the cool air conditioning while waiting for a possible Leanne Strong sighting," Dad says. "Ready to go home?"

"On the off chance you do have unwanted visitors...why don't you come to our house instead?" asks Mrs. Dalisay. "We'll hide Leanne in our backyard."

~

"Do you think I'd make the cheer squad?" Sami flips around the backyard, showing me a cartwheel and a handspring. "If not, I might take up ski jumping this winter since I'm not dancing anymore."

Mr. Dalisay chokes on his sip of wine. "Why not try skydiving while you're at it? Race car driving, too."

Sami makes a face. "Gotcha, Dad. No ski jumping." She flits over to me. "Nice bracelet, Leanne. Is that your birthday gift from Braeden?"

My face warms like the surface of the sun. "No, I've had this for a while."

Sami glances at her scowling brother and claps her hand over her mouth. "Oooh. Sorry. Are you two still fighting?"

Braeden aims a sharp glance at his sister. Our parents' conversation grinds to a halt. Collectively, they stare at us, waiting for an answer. Braeden sets his glass on the picnic table and stands. "I'm finished here. Want to take a walk?"

We wrap around the house, following the reverse path of my June eighth escape route. Solar lights flick on in the neighbors' yards. A peaceful stillness lingers in the air as summer draws to a close.

Braeden reaches for my hand.

"So, has Harper stopped by lately?" I ask, hoping to sound casual.

Braeden scrunches his face into one of his signature scowls. "Harper never talks to me. She calls Sami. They're friends again."

"Really?" I grind to a halt. "I mean, that's great for Sami. But..."

We cross the street, my unfinished sentence hanging in the air between us.

"But what?" Braeden asks, stepping up on the sidewalk.

"I saw you together, outside of your house. After you told me that you needed space." He pauses in front of the gate to my backyard, waiting for me to finish. "I thought you sent me away so you could be with her."

He looks at me strangely. "Why would I want to be with her? We broke up almost a year ago."

I reach past him and unlatch the gate. Braeden pulls it open and we slip into the backyard. "Harper knew Em. My mom thought Sami should talk to someone who remembers all the girl stuff they did together."

"Your mom's right," I agree. "Sami needs that."

"Anyway," he continues, on a roll now, "why did you give Sami your medal? You never took it off."

"I-I thought she needed it." I stumble a bit, surprised he noticed such a small detail about me. "Why did you stop coming to work?"

Braeden lifts his eyes to the sky. "I wanted to work through some stuff. I went back to my therapist. My parents told me I had to, but they were right. We all went together and…talked things out."

I squeeze his hand and he squeezes back.

"Did it help?"

"Yeah. I mean, a little bit. It's just going to take time."

But he seems different today. More relaxed. Closer to the smiling pictures of him in Sami's memory book.

"Hey," I say, tugging on his hand. "Thanks for coming today."

His mouth slants into a half-smile. "I wouldn't miss a chance to hear Leanne Strong talk about her miracle. You were awesome, by the way. That was a stellar speech."

I cringe at the memory. "My dad helped me write it."

"But the words were yours. I could tell."

"Oh, like you know me so well," I say, trying to lighten what's quickly becoming a heavy discussion.

His chin drops and he stares at the grass. "I do. At least, I think I do."

"Then why did you…leave me?" My voice catches and I feel the burn in my eyes. When I hitch in a breath, Braeden wraps an arm around my back and draws me into an awkward embrace. But the warmth of his touch calms my agitation.

"I'm sorry, Leanne. To be honest, I wasn't sure if I was ready to be happy."

I flinch and then steel myself. "Are you ready now?"

His other hand slides around my waist, drawing me closer. "Yes. I think I am."

The wind whips my hair in front of my face and I reach up to tuck a stray lock behind my ear. "Okay." I steady myself and keep going. "What do you want to do, then? Besides walk up and down Chestnut Street?"

With a quiet laugh, he spins me around until I'm facing the deck behind my house. "I want to sit on that swing thing over there and listen to you tell me what I missed at work the last three weeks."

A rush of emotion flows out from my heart, filling me with joy. The air around us hums, like angels are singing and birds are chirping only for me and Braeden. We climb the steps onto the deck and take our usual seats in the glider.

"So, does this mean we're friends again?" I brush my fingers over his arm.

Braeden scowls, but not in a mean way. "I wanted us to be together. You know that, right?"

"Yes, even when we weren't talking, I knew you still cared," I say. He helped me find Callie. "But saying you *wanted* to be with me won't fix everything between us."

He leans back on the glider, setting the seat in motion. "When I saw you running from that reporter on June eighth...for the first time since Emeline died, the world seemed lighter. For a second, I forgot how much I hated myself, and it scared me. I wanted to feel heavy. I wasn't ready to stop feeling..."

"Sad?" I ask. "You weren't ready to move past the sadness?"

He runs his hand through his hair. "If I moved past Em's death, I felt like I was forgetting her. Moving here, meeting people who never knew her. Anyway, I acted like a jerk, hoping you would get fed up with me. But you never got mad. I tried to push you away for your own good. That didn't work, either."

"So what now?"

Our eyes meet. He looks away first, running his hand through his hair. "Now? It's your call. I just want to tell you that I missed you every day, Leanne. Seeing you is the one thing I look forward to."

I shift my weight and the glider rocks. "I missed you, too. I wanted to help you, but I didn't know how. So I let you go."

"Don't feel bad about it." He reaches for my hand and laces our fingers together. "I needed the time on my own. I'll never forget what happened to Emeline. My part in it. But, I think I can find a way to move on."

For a long time, we sit and swing, letting the darkness hold us together.

"I watched you," I whisper. "With Sami and your parents. You took care of them, even when you didn't realize you were doing it. Maybe you couldn't move on, because you were waiting for them to move on first."

A slow breath eases from his chest and he holds my hand tighter. "When Sami got sick—and we went back to the hospital—I was scared, Leanne. Instead of showing you how afraid I was, I shut us down." He picks up our joined hands and studies them for a long minute. "I need to make it up to you. Sami agreed."

My shoulders tense. "You talked to Sami about us?"

Recalling the conversation, Braeden looks amused. "Most of the time she talked and I listened. The past couple of weeks, we cooked up a plan to surprise you at the dedication."

"I was hoping you'd come, but I didn't believe it until I saw you at the shrine."

He smiles to himself. "I read some of the articles she cut out for your scrapbook. Those scientific experts are seriously aggravated when they can't explain something. You freaked out the entire medical profession." He reaches into his pocket and pulls out a small box. "This is your birthday present from me. Sorry it's late, but I had to wait for it to come in the mail."

"I know you took the pictures in the scrapbook," I say, refusing to take the box when he holds it out. "That was enough."

He takes my hand and wraps my fingers around his gift. "No, it wasn't. This belongs to you."

Inside, I find a shiny new medal hanging from a silver chain.

"Brought to you by the Sisters of Saint Piera," Braeden says. "I wrote them a letter – because apparently they don't answer emails or texts—and asked for a replacement. I don't think Sami plans to return your original."

"She can keep it. Forever." My hands shake as I slip the chain around my neck. With the weight of the medal resting against my chest, I feel like everything is right with the world again. "Thank you, Braeden." I press my lips lightly against his cheek.

He drops his hand to my hip, holding me close. "You're welcome."

A smile plays at his lips and I wonder what's coming next.

"Just say it," I tell him.

He stops the glider and the entire world seems to freeze in place, waiting. "I think I might be falling in love with you, Leanne."

The earnest look on his face pulls a smile from me. "Did Callie tell you to say that?"

He shakes his head, confused. "I haven't talked to Callie."

"The night we picked her up at Jake's house, she watched us from the porch and noticed how hard it was for us to stay away from each other."

He sinks back in the glider. "So I was obvious, huh?"

"You weren't obvious to me."

He leans forward, his mouth close to mine. When we kiss,

I expect to feel his hesitation, but instead I only sense his desire to make things right between us.

"Do you believe me now?" he asks.

I raise my hand and touch my lips, already missing the feel of him. "I think love is more than kissing."

"You're probably right. How about this?" He takes both of my hands in his. "I love you, Leanne. Not just because you're a constant source of miracles. I love you because you truly care about my family. You didn't run away from Sami when she needed a friend."

"How could I run away?" I ask, hearing my voice shake. "I needed her, too. Both of you."

He brushes his fingers over my cheek before he kisses me again. I loop my arms around his neck and intensify the kiss, showing him the truth about my feelings for him.

After a while he eases back. "Also, you should know I think you're extremely beautiful."

I laugh. "Not really."

He places his hand under my chin and forces me to look at him. "Yes, you are. Inside and out. But I said all that other stuff so you wouldn't think I was only attracted to you because you're hot."

My heart starts to pound in my chest and I look away before daring to say, "I might have noticed certain um, physical attributes, about you, too."

He breathes out a laugh. "So we're even. And, you'll let me know when you're ready to go out with me? I guess at some point I should ask you to be my girlfriend. Sami keeps bugging me about putting a label on us."

I nestle into my favorite spot, leaning against his chest and gazing up into his dark brown eyes. "If you're ready to try this again, so am I. Oh, and in case you're wondering, I love you, too. You're also extremely beautiful – inside and out."

"Ah, now you feel like you have to say something nice," he says, but his smile melts my heart.

We spend an hour gliding together, catching up on our days apart. When the sun sinks below the treetops and my parents call to us from inside the house, Braeden kisses me one last time.

"Today was the perfect day," I say, lingering in his arms. "I don't want it to end."

To which he replies, "I can't wait for tomorrow because I'll be with you."

About the Author

Jennifer DiGiovanni is the author of contemporary and light fantasy books for teens. In addition to reading and writing, she loves to hike and run outdoors, when the weather cooperates. She also enjoys traveling and trying new activities, from archery to video games to guitar, all in the name of book research.

Jennifer recently returned to her home in Pennsylvania, after living in Canada for two years.

To learn more about Jennifer and her books, visit her website at www.jenniferdigiovanni.com.

Acknowledgments

Thank you to everyone who helped me bring this story to life, especially my teachers who encouraged my love of books and writing. I still have papers with your notes written in the margins. Also, thanks to my parents who taught me about faith and have never failed to support my writing journey. I'd also like to send a big thank you to my husband and children, for their continuing faith in me.

My gratitude goes out to everyone at Vinspire for working so hard to create this book. Thank you to the Vinspire authors for welcoming me into your group. And lastly, I can never express how thankful I am for my friends in the book community who read early versions (or multiple versions) of this story and offered their feedback. I couldn't have finished this book without your help and support.

The author gratefully acknowledges the use of the following Trademarks:

Keurig - Keurig Green Mountain, Inc. CORPORATION DELAWARE 53 South Avenue Burlington MASSACHUSETTS 01803

K-Cup - Keurig Green Mountain, Inc. CORPORATION DELAWARE 33 Coffee Lane Waterbury VERMONT 05676

YouTube - Google LLC LIMITED LIABILITY COMPANY DELAWARE 1600 Amphitheatre Parkway Mountain View CALIFORNIA 94043

Teen Vouge - Advance Magazine Publishers Inc. CORPORATION NEW YORK One World Trade Center New York NEW YORK 100072915

Dear Reader

If you enjoyed reading *Miracle Girl*, I would appreciate it if you would help others enjoy this book, too. Here are some of the ways you can help spread the word:

Lend it. This book is lending enabled so please share it with a friend.

Recommend it. Help other readers find this book by recommending it to friends, readers' groups, book clubs, and discussion forums.

Share it. Let other readers know you've read the book by positing a note to your social media account and/or your Goodreads account.

Review it. Please tell others why you liked this book by reviewing it on your favorite ebook site.

Everything you do to help others learn about my book is greatly appreciated!

Jennifer DiGiovanni

Plan Your Next Escape!
What's Your Reading Pleasure?

Whether it's captivating historical romance, intriguing mysteries, young adult romance, illustrated children's books, or uplifting love stories, Vinspire Publishing has the adventure for you!

For a complete listing of books available, visit our website at www.vinspirepublishing.com.

Like us on Facebook at
www.facebook.com/VinspirePublishing

Follow us on Twitter at
www.twitter.com/vinspire2004

and follow our blog for details of our upcoming releases, giveaways, author insights, and more!

www.vinspirepublishingblog.com.

We are your travel guide to your next adventure!

CPSIA information can be obtained
at www.ICGtesting.com
Printed in the USA
LVHW111734050320
649104LV00005B/885